MW00937479

UNHOLY SILENCE, JOURNAL OF A WHISTLEBLOWER
Third Edition
Copyright © 2013
Patrick J. Flynn
All rights reserved.

ISBN: 978-1-105-01497-0

Unholy Silence

Journal of a Whistleblower
Patrick J. Flynn

In a serious emergency when the innocent
are in danger, silence is as evil as the
victimization itself.

Editor's Notes:

The content of this writing is painstakingly accurate. However, where deemed necessary, names of individuals and entities have been changed to give every opportunity for healing and reparation.

Chapter Eight contains some extremely explicit text which is necessary in context.

Introduction:

So I now say to you: You are Peter and on this rock I will build my church. And the gates of the underworld can never overpower it. Matt 16:18

It is so very important that something be made clear from the onset. It is clear that Jesus Christ has promised that the gates of Hell would not prevail against His Church. That is truth in its purest form. Jesus did not promise, however, that the power of Hell would not destroy faith, deceive and consume human souls, and significantly damage the mission of the Church because He knew that it would.

A tremendous amount of material has been written, studied and revealed concerning the suffering and pain of the direct victims of the global clergy sex abuse crisis, and rightly so. It has been rather rare, however, to hear from the perspective of some of the other victims. Like the direct victims, whistleblowers are innocent. Unlike most direct victims, they are vilified, persecuted and attacked indefinitely being denied the restraint often afforded to children.

It must be understood that at this writing, there are faithful cardinals, bishops, church officials, clergy and religious, seminarians, and lay people. All of these dedicated people are of good will. They are praying and working hard to help our embattled Church recognize, deal with, and heal from the horrible crisis of clergy sexual abuse. They do this today as they have done throughout the centuries during times of suffering in the Catholic Church.

Likewise for the past several decades, as throughout the centuries, there have been and still are shocking numbers of guilty and unrepentant cardinals, bishops, church officials, clergy and religious, seminarians, and lay people. They are still active in destroying faith worldwide. They are still lying and covering up the truth. They are still remaining silent while innocence is violated. If you disagree with this, you are denying reality. In that case you should probably just put this book down, give it away, or throw it away. This writing, while documenting one local story fearlessly attempts to pierce the veil that covers sin and break the silence that is ruining people's lives.

If we are given the opportunity to look back on this time hundreds of years from now, we will have cause to identify this period as perhaps the most difficult trial of the Catholic Church in its impressive history. The crisis of sexual misconduct, most notably homosexual abuse of minors by clergy and the failure of church authority to appropriately respond have ravaged Christianity and damaged countless souls. In properly dealing with this we should have learned at least one major lesson thus far: Anything but the truth is harmful and dangerous and silence is the foundation upon which evil builds its infrastructure.

The cover up of the clergy sex abuse crisis is at the root of all the conflict. Traditionally what has occurred was that offending clergy have been whisked off to different parishes with their previous behavior silenced by church leadership. Once there, the clergy members preyed upon new victims. This cover up technique has of late been discovered and exposed. It is not possible for guilty bishops and church officials to do this any longer on a large scale while evading detection. To be quite honest, they can no longer financially afford to take such risks. Shamefully the only motivation for many church leaders to act against the crisis has been fear of financial ruin. Regardless of the exposure of the problem, cover up is still considered necessary by corrupt leadership. This is because a good number of them are personally guilty of the same revolting behavior as the accused priests, and the offending priests are not ignorant of that fact. It is reasonable to assume that a great deal of closed door meetings are taking place whereas the accused are sending the message to leadership that they're not going to go down alone. This would prevent even a repentant bishop or cardinal from doing the right thing for fear of wide-scale exposition of corruption and ensuing personal implications. Therefore, cover up is still alive and well and silence rules the day and buys the time.

Now, let's consider the past several years and the revelation of the global crisis. Obviously something had to be done to convince the world that this problem would be addressed and brought under control. Several years ago the authority figures convened and asked us to believe that a new policy of "zero tolerance" was being implemented. With all due respect, the new policy of zero tolerance is for the most part the joke of the century.

Consider this analogy: Police corruption evolves to the point in a major city where it cannot be denied and something must be done about it. The governor of the state demands the mayor do his job and remedy this. The mayor meets with the cops and they develop a plan. Together they call a press conference and proclaim to the state leader and all the citizens, "We have a new policy of zero tolerance regarding corruption and we'll take care of the problem, rest assured."

Would you feel safe if this were your city? Knowing how insidious corruption and foul play can be and how it develops and spreads through ranks of authority, would you feel that the same leadership who fostered and permitted the corruption would be trustworthy to stop it?

Why is it then that we seemed satisfied that the current leaders in the church would end the crisis? How could we believe that guilty bishops would hold guilty priests accountable? They won't because they can't. Only holy bishops and cardinals can stop the abuse and its cover up. Only God knows how many holy bishops and cardinals are really on the job right now. The harsh reality is that most of the guilty cardinals, bishops and priests are going to have to die off before we emerge from this horror. That is the simple nature of the deadly cocktail of power, sin, denial and cover up. What all too often can be found slithering through the marbled halls of our courts and legislatures also slithers through the pews of our cathedrals.

So, we are not really on the downhill regarding the clergy sex abuse crisis. It is not just a matter of days or weeks before we have the problem under control. It will take many years for us to rise from these ashes. But, rise we must.

This crisis is particularly horrible because it violates faith itself. The vulnerability necessary for real faith to exist predisposes us to the pain we feel when our church leaders disappoint us. We share a portion of the blame for this in the unfair exaltation with which we shower these men. When they inevitably reveal their fallible humanity, and in far too many cases, mortal sin, our iconic image of the hero is smashed. All too often, we are prone to bestow onto clergy members themselves that which God alone deserves. When we give to others even a small portion of that which is God's, we will be disappointed. Human beings disappoint one another. We always have and we always will. That is a sad unavoidable aspect of our nature. The leadership of the Catholic Church, however, has every moral, legal and decent obligation to address the tragedy of the fallen priesthood. This particular story unfortunately gives evidence to their failure to do just that.

This compilation focuses on one local chapter of this tragedy. The manner in which it occurred, developed and is playing out is not unlike similar episodes of its kind around the world. It is a true story of behavior, discovery, accusations, denial, investigation, pride, suspicion, rejection, vindication, heartbreak, sadness, fear, disappointment, love, and frustration. This litany of human drama is horrifyingly inevitable when a faith community has its heart lacerated virtually overnight and its spiritual foundation shaken.

The key individuals active in this story are not necessarily good or bad people. They are human beings who are facing tragedy. They are doing what all humans do in the face of heartbreak. They are responding. Human beings by virtue of our vast diversity all deal with conflict in different manners. It is inevitable that in responding, some involved will make honest mistakes. Some are beset with personal issues that interfere with honest evaluation. It is also inevitable that in situations that are this serious, some will also choose the path of malice. We all have opinions, issues and experiences that affect how we will respond to painful situations. In this story, relationships are fractured, emotions are released, gossip races and trust wanes. This is all made possible by a campaign of silence, the option of weak leaders who rather than courageously address the crisis, simply withdraw and hope for an evaporation of the controversy. Before we can begin to deal with all of these complexities in any occurrence of this nature there is emergency action that must take place. *The innocent must be protected at all costs.* This is first and foremost above all concerns.

As in any injury, we can rise from the ashes wiser, stronger, less dependent on the world and more faithful to our Divine Master. Around the world, clergy and laity who have remained faithful hope and pray for healing. May God heed these fervent appeals soon.

This journal is not a critical condemnation of Father Thomas or any other same-sex attracted individual. It is a documentation of a difficult and necessary course of actions heart-wrenchingly undertaken to protect innocent teenage boys from predatory abuse. In this instance, the likelihood of this abuse was predisposed due to Father Thomas' desires, his denial of the implications and dangers of disordered interest in young men and the refusal of church authority figures to address the patterns and specific situations of this and other similar cases both locally and worldwide.

I believe it is appropriate to document here the teaching of the Catholic Church regarding homosexuality. I not only accept this teaching, but embrace it as divinely inspired wisdom. Christians have an obligation to understand and practice mercy and compassion upon those who suffer with same-sex attraction.

The Catechism of the Catholic Church:

> 2357
>
> Homosexuality refers to relations between men or between women who experience an exclusive or predominant sexual attraction toward persons of the same sex. It has taken a great variety of forms through the centuries and in different cultures. Its psychological genesis remains largely unexplained. Basing itself

on Sacred Scripture, which presents homosexual acts as acts of grave depravity, tradition has always declared that "homosexual acts are intrinsically disordered." They are contrary to the natural law. They close the sexual act to the gift of life. They do not proceed from a genuine affective and sexual complementarity. Under no circumstances can they be approved.

2358

The number of men and women who have deep-seated homosexual tendencies is not negligible. This inclination, which is objectively disordered, constitutes for most of them a trial. They must be accepted with respect, compassion, and sensitivity. Every sign of unjust discrimination in their regard should be avoided. These persons are called to fulfill God's will in their lives and, if they are Christians, to unite to the sacrifice of the Lord's Cross the difficulties they may encounter from their condition.

2359

Homosexual persons are called to chastity. By the virtues of self-mastery that teach them inner freedom, at times by the support of disinterested friendship, by prayer and sacramental grace, they can and should gradually and resolutely approach Christian perfection.

We must come to understand the inner struggle same-sex attracted individuals endure. The genesis of their desires as outlined in the Catechism still remains unexplained. However, emerging psychological and behavioral science is casting more light on the reasons people experience same-sex attraction. Men and women are not born genetically destined to be attracted to the same gender. Despite assertions and beliefs in this concept, no science can document such a notion. According to research and decades-long case studies by the National Association for Research and Therapy of Homosexuality (NARTH), same-sex attraction has little or nothing to do with sex or innate attraction rather with the psycho-sexualization of traumatic or abnormal events or patterns during the developing years. Some of the most common scenarios or events among same-sex attracted individuals include but are not limited to absent or weak fathers, dominating or cruel mothers, abandonment, sexual abuse and molestation as children. It is precisely the psycho-sexualization itself and the process of its development that still eludes definitive explanation.

Legally the sexual abuse of minors is Pedophilia. However, the psychological community separates the disorder with puberty as the dividing factor. Pedophilia is the disorder whereas the sexual attraction of the adult is directed toward pre-pubescent children. Ephebophilia is the attraction directed toward post-pubescent children.

In the case of Fr. Thomas as in the vast majority of all known cases of clergy sexual misconduct, we are dealing with homosexual Ephebophilia.

The Catholic seminaries had a solemn obligation before God to keep men with sexually disordered issues from becoming priests. Many, even some within the Church question why this should be so. They have argued that a homosexual man is just as capable of living a celibate life as a heterosexual man. Capable yes, but certainly not as likely. Research and studies clearly indicate substantially higher levels of promiscuity and sexual preoccupation among homosexuals than heterosexuals.

Psychiatrist, Dr. Richard Fitzgibbons, a consultant to the Vatican Congregation for Clergy and a leading expert with more than 35 years of clinical experience treating priests and others with same-sex attraction said in a recent interview with regard to homosexuality in the priesthood, "Narcissism – a personality disorder in which an insatiable need for admiration often leads to attention-seeking behavior – is prevalent among men who struggle with homosexuality. This conflict results in a need to draw attention to his own personality in the Liturgy rather than to surrender his personal identity in favor of Christ."

While narcissistic behavior certainly isn't the exclusive franchise of homosexual persons, Dr. Fitzgibbons' insights speak directly to the reason why homosexual men are ill-suited for the priesthood.[1]

The primary sexual interest toward minors is even more egregious in this regard. Father Thomas should have been cared for and assisted with his inner struggle with proper ministry but his ordination to the sacred priesthood was a serious mistake.

Dr. James Hitchcock, Professor of History at St. Loius University writes:

> "The sexual orientation of a priest or of a future priest has to be of concern to his superiors, whose task it is to discern whether he is leading a celibate life. If he is, it is no one else's business. **But if orientation leads to action, it becomes everyone's business.**"[4]

It is true that this book is a study of the crisis presented through one man's experience. But, please remember, this man has walked this horrible path for years. No one on Earth knows more concerning the details of this localized crisis than the individual who at this moment is typing this sentence. Additionally, many observations and examples of a psychological and behavioral nature are presented to help the reader understand the complexity of the crisis. These do not come through a framework of personal scientific credentials but rather through substantial real-life experience, common sense and verifiable research.

Dedication:

This book is dedicated to my family, collateral innocent victims who have remained courageous and steadfast in the face of hurtful and slanderous persecution.

It is dedicated to those men and women of the laity and clergy who remain faithful and prayerfully committed to helping the Catholic Church to emerge strengthened, and healed from one of the most devastating and heartbreaking scandals of her history.

It is dedicated to the repentance, forgiveness, and reparation of the offending clergy who have fallen into grave sin, to the hierarchy who failed to protect the innocent while assisting the offenders and to the healing of the those members of the laity who consciously or unconsciously enable the guilty, and join them in their denial.

It is dedicated above all, to Our Lord Jesus Christ who is at this moment cleansing his church of its sin, and bringing us more fully into the springtime of the new evangelization in preparation for his second coming.

Background

Holy Cross Parish is a Catholic Church in Michigan. Catholic Churches all over the world are considerably independent in that the pastor of each parish, a Catholic priest, has full solitary authority over every aspect of his parish under Canon law. Catholic churches are, however, also dependent in that they are subject to a Catholic bishop both doctrinally and governmentally as part of a geographical region called a diocese. Holy Cross Parish is one of the 96 churches in the Diocese of Hamburg in Michigan. During this scandal the Bishop of the Diocese was Carl Martin. The diocese can be considered a parent company to the parish. Both the parish and the diocese are businesses. Both take in resources, make expenditures, and hire employees. Under Canon law, any issues that transcend the authority of the local pastor are to be handled by the authority of the Bishop's office. For example, in the Diocese of Hamburg, a local pastor has full authority to spend up to $50,000 of the parish's resources on virtually whatever he wishes. Any expenditure above that amount requires the written approval of the Bishop.

I was employed as Business Manager for Holy Cross Parish. I am a layman, sole supporter of my wife, Laura and then seven children. My position at Holy Cross was created in 2000 as a means to shift the burden of business details from the shoulders of the Pastor, Father Wesley Thomas, affording him the opportunity to focus solely on the spiritual and Sacramental needs of the faithful. It is important to note that under Canon Law, the pastor still must exercise ultimate decisional authority on all substantial matters. After learning that I was selected for the position, I moved my pregnant wife and my six children from Jacksonville, Florida up to Brighton to accept my new job. My first day was September 11, exactly one year prior to the historically infamous day that the world will never forget. The parish was very welcoming upon our arrival. We had many instant friends. Laura was homeschooling the children. The parish had at the time over forty homeschooling families.

Father Thomas' past – a puzzling journey

Our Pastor and my boss, Fr. Thomas was a native of Lansing, Michigan. He was an only child who, while I knew him, seldom spoke of his parents. He became a school teacher and worked at a high school in Lansing. He then converted to the Catholic faith. After serving his preparatory deaconate at a parish in Brighton, Michigan, Father then went to Germany where he was ordained a priest at age forty. He returned to Michigan again five months later and began serving as Parochial Vicar at the same Brighton parish. Father then served a period at two other parishes in Michigan until 1981 when he once again left the United States to study in Europe and the Holy Land. During the five years abroad, Father adopted a sixteen year-old Palestinian boy. Father and his adopted son returned to Michigan in 1986. He then worked as a Chaplain in the Hamburg Diocese at a Catholic high school for boys. In 1989, Father Thomas once again returned to Germany and served as Pastor of a Parish in Wurzburg. In 1998, he returned to the United States yet again and led a missionary church in McLean, Virginia. Father returned to Michigan and the Diocese of Hamburg in 1999 when he was assigned as Pastor of Holy Cross.

Father Bill, as he was known and I seemed to work quite well together. A concern did surface, however, rather soon whereas Father seemed to be increasingly unavailable to the staff and the parishioners. As time progressed, the problem worsened. Ultimately, the fact was that Father Bill, rather than using my position for its intended purpose of freeing himself for ministry, was instead using the position as an excuse to virtually disappear. His office at the church was always empty and locked. Father lived in the parish rectory, a self-contained home on the parish grounds. Although Father maintained a study in the rectory, it would have been very rare to find him there conducting valid parish ministry. Another obviously growing problem was that Father was carelessly spending parish money on himself and his rectory without any real concern for existing parish budgets and the need for moderation.

It is noteworthy to mention that the parish at large was willing to overlook these human "imperfections" because Father was telling most of them what they longed to hear. Father was using lots of candles, incense, bells, and Latin liturgies. He had an altar rail constructed in the sanctuary. At times he could be seen wearing a full length cassock. He had a prison ministry counseling and bringing the Sacraments to incarcerated boys. He participated in mission trips to Mexico and the Dominican Republic. He permitted the establishment of Eucharistic Adoration at the parish. He spoke against homosexual "marriage" and abortion. Father looked like and sounded like a very effective Catholic parish leader. Understandably, this would present difficulty for some, if not most of the parish to accept the possibility of conflict regarding Father's public ministry and his private behavior.

My duties as Business Manager made it necessary for me to sit on both the Parish Finance Council and the Parish Pastoral Leadership Council, more commonly referred to as simply, the Parish Council. It was Father's obligation to also preside on the Finance Council, but he never attended the meetings. As time progressed, the members of the two councils became increasingly frustrated with Father Bill's disconnection from both good parish financial stewardship and his disconnection from the faithful as well. People began to resign from the councils out of frustration, and finding replacements for them became difficult to impossible.

Chapter One
Fourteenth Century Sobering Relevance to Twenty-First Century Reality

Astonishingly, the global clergy sexual misbehavior, while recently redeveloped in devastating intensity, is not a new problem. Why would it be? Has not temptation and sin been a particular tool of the evil one since the beginning of the human race? St. Catherine of Siena, Doctor of the Church recorded her communication with the Almighty over 700 years ago:

> "I have told you, dearest daughter, something of the reverence that ought to be given my anointed ones no matter how sinful they may be. For reverence neither is nor should be given them for what they are in themselves, but only for the authority I have entrusted to them. The sacramental mystery cannot be lessened or divided by their sinfulness. Therefore, your reverence for them should never fail— not for their own sake, but because of the treasure of the blood."

> "For those who are not corrected and those who do not correct are like members beginning to rot...But those who are in authority today do not do this. In fact they pretend not to see ...They will never correct persons of any importance...They will, however, correct the little people ... And do you know why? Because the root of selfish love is alive in them, and this is the source of their perverse slavish fear...They believe they can succeed through injustice, by not reproving the sins of their subjects... Another reason they will not correct others is that they themselves are living in the same or greater sins. They sense that the same guilt envelops them, so they cast aside fervor and confidence and, chained by slavish fear, pretend they do not see."

> **"I want to show you the wretchedness of their lives, so that you and my other servants will have the more reason to offer me humble and constant prayer for them**. No matter where you turn, to diocesan or religious, priests or bishops, lowly or great, young or old, you see nothing but sin...the filth of deadly sin."

> **"They get up in the morning with their minds contaminated and their bodies corrupt. After spending the night bedded**

down with deadly sin they go to celebrate Mass! O tabernacles of the devil!"

"No, these wretches not only do not restrain their weakness; they make it worse by committing that cursed unnatural sin...The stench reaches even up to me, supreme Purity, and is so hateful to me that for this sin alone five cities were struck down by my divine judgment. For my divine justice could no longer tolerate it, so despicable to me is this abominable sin."

Concerning the active practice of homosexuality, Catherine hears the Almighty Father say: "How abominable this sin is to me in any person. Now imagine how much more hateful it is in those I have called to live celibately."

"And how can those who are so sinful bring their subjects to justice and reproach them for their sins? They cannot, for their own sins have left them bereft of any enthusiasm or zeal for holy justice...And sometimes when they recognize that these religious are incarnate devils, they send them from one monastery to the next to those who are incarnate devils like themselves. Thus each corrupts the other... Superiors are the cause of these and many other evils because they do not keep their eyes on their subjects...they pretend not to see their wretched behavior."

This was recorded over 700 years ago. This is a sobering reminder that we battle with principalities and powers rather than flesh and blood. Throughout twenty-one centuries, the perfect and divinely instituted Church of Jesus Christ has been both cared for and polluted by fallible, sinful man. Jesus Christ knew the heart and mind of man. Man was the being of his own creation. One must assume that Jesus knew what he was doing when he left his Bride, the Church in man's care. Jesus sealed the protection of the Church with his promise. But obviously the freely committed misdeeds of man and the devastating effects those misdeeds produce would need to be courageously identified, addressed, and corrected many times since the Holy Spirit descended upon the Apostles and established the Church around the year 33 AD. Jesus left us the Sacrament of Reconciliation to give us strength, forgiveness and a continually new resolve. So here we find ourselves at the beginning of the 21st Century with yet another

19

tremendous cross. We behold a devastating and worldwide crisis combining age-old sin, temptation and human fallibility with new and horrifyingly destructive details. It seems that a great evil that has always existed at some level throughout the centuries has in most recent decades grown to overwhelming and catastrophic proportions.

Chapter Two
A Tragic Discovery

It was July of 2004. Father Bill called me from his car on his cell phone. He was frustrated because the anti-virus program on his computer in the rectory study was malfunctioning. He asked me to go up to the rectory and see if I could get to the bottom of the problem. I arrived in the rectory study and logged on to Father's computer. Father's password was "holiness." Father was protective over his computer and had it configured to automatically log off following any brief time with no activity. I do recall a reappearing error message issuing from the anti-virus application. I do not recall the exact message, only that the solution was not immediately at hand. I opened up Internet Explorer to try to find some remedy on the internet. I remember clicking on the address bar's down arrow which revealed recent internet activity. Near the top of the list that appeared was an MSN search, "gay male sex." I was momentarily stunned.

For a moment, I didn't quite know what to think. I remember at that same time, Father was complaining from time to time that he was getting a considerable amount of nasty spam emails. I went into his Outlook Express and sure enough found a large number of extreme, and explicitly titled emails. What troubled me about this discovery was that because they were not bold in font, apparently they had been opened. I recall telling Father that the very last thing he should do was to ever open any obvious spam emails, lest the problem would only grow.

I went back to my office and wondered what to do about what I discovered. I don't even recall whether or not I was able to resolve the anti-virus problem. Father never did tell me that he was still receiving these errors.

I began to think about many things in light of this discovery. Father did have a teenage boy from the parish on the part time payroll to do work at the rectory. The thought did occur to me that perhaps it could have been him who conducted the search. But this did not settle logically as a real possibility for several reasons.

First of all, Kyle almost never showed up for work and when he did, he was almost always outside. Also, would Kyle have Father's password and would he have opened up Father's emails? It was of course possible but just did not seem likely. What was now very troubling were the many subtle and not so subtle indications over time that might have suggested that privately, Father was struggling with same-sex desires and temptations.

About a month before Kyle started working at the rectory, Father had employed another teenage boy from the parish. Alex had worked at the rectory for about a year until his mother abruptly ended his employment. Unlike Kyle, Alex not only performed odd jobs at the rectory, but also hung out there quite often, sometimes daily. He would do his homework and frequently watch TV. Alex, not unlike many sixteen year-olds was having a difficult time with his parents and his home was within walking distance. What was disturbing about this was that Father was fixated on the boy. He spoke of him constantly. He would pick him up from school, take him shopping, to events or out to eat on many occasions. Father once brought Alex and one of his friends up to his cottage in Northern Michigan for a weekend. I, along with the Parish Pastoral Coordinator, Michael Wilson attempted to warn Father Thomas about the perceived impropriety of this relationship at a time when many other measures were being taken at the church to increase personal safety and security. We installed windows on all office doors, established policy preventing one-on-one mixed gender meetings, and Father himself sectioned off his confessional behind a locked door. This was to prevent any face-to-face confessions and thereby eliminating any false accusations or misunderstandings. Father dismissed our warnings concerning his relationship with Alex. He told us that the teen needed him and was blessed to have a peaceful refuge at the rectory away from his difficult home life. Since this was prior to my discovery, Wilson and I essentially had no reason but to give Father the benefit of the doubt concerning the ministerial purpose of the relationship.

When Alex was hired, Father Thomas asked me to set up a user account for the boy on his computer in the rectory study. He wanted Alex to have a separate identity and password to log on. I was also instructed to provide the boy with a cell phone at the church's expense.

Father used his position on the staff and the Board of Directors of Bishop Gabriel Catholic High School to help Alex gain admission there. Father went so far as to state that he would pay the teenager's tuition himself if he had to.

Father told me of the tensions the boy was facing at home and blamed Alex's mother for being too restrictive and oppressive with her son. Apparently during the time that Alex was visiting the rectory, his grades and demeanor did seem to improve according to Father. Father credited this improvement on the fact that the boy had found a positive and non-threatening atmosphere at the rectory. Father informed me that Alex's mother approached Father one day after Mass and thanked him for taking such pastoral interest in her son. She mentioned that this was a blessing for her family and it was too bad that Father wasn't around when her older children were going through their difficult teen years. Of course, events in the near future would reveal a much more troubling aspect to Father's regard for Alex.

One day without warning the relationship between Father and Alex was abruptly ended. According to Father, the boy's mother confronted him and told him to stay away from her family. Alex was no longer employed by the church, and he was never seen at the rectory again. Father said he had no idea why the mother would do such a thing, and hinted that she was emotionally unstable.

I did not know this at the time, but Alex's parents filed a formal complaint with The Diocese of Hamburg regarding Father's relationship with their son.

In August of 2004, I was able to discover while conducting further work on Father's computer, that 8 of the 25 most recent web searches were of a sexually suspicious nature.

Soon after this, my family and I left for a two-week vacation in Florida. I had not shared my discovery with anyone including my wife. During the vacation, I left and told Laura that I was going onto the mainland to run some errands. I headed for a Catholic Church in Melbourne Beach that I had seen a few days before. I was hoping that the pastor would be available. I believed this to be an inspired opportunity since I did not know this pastor, he did not know me or Father Thomas and we were a safe thousand miles from Holy Cross. It was important to me that any counsel sought at this stage be anonymous. In the event that this was some terrible misunderstanding, Father's reputation could suffer badly. The pastor of the large Florida church was available to see me. I proceeded to tell the priest what I had found on Father Bill's computer. I also told him about the situation with Alex at the rectory. The 60ish legally blind priest expressed how potentially dangerous this could all be especially in light of the huge unfolding clergy sexual abuse scandal that was rocking the Catholic Church. To this day I do not know that pastor's name. He told me that as difficult as it may be, I was obliged to tell Father Bill about my discovery when I returned to Michigan.

Around August 20, I had occasion to be up at the rectory. Father was there. I asked him to come into the study for a moment. I sat down at his computer and pulled down his recent searches in his Internet Explorer. He looked at the contents of the list and seemed instantly stunned. He said, "what the hell is that?" I told him that I had discovered this while working on his computer before vacation. He asked me who had access to his computer. I reminded him now that Alex was long gone, the only ones that have access were he and I. Father reiterated that he knew nothing about the searches and was clueless as to their appearance.

I had done what the priest in Florida told me I was obligated to do. It did not make logical sense that Father knew nothing of the searches, but I had brought it to his attention nonetheless. I gave Father Bill the benefit of the doubt. I, however, decided that I would check whenever I was given the opportunity and just see if any activity of this nature continued. I believed I had a moral obligation to do so for the sake of the parish children. I was

24

content in my conscience that if I discovered no more activity like this, that I would tell no one about it, ever. It was quite a while before I had the opportunity to be back up at the rectory without Father being present. The devastating reality was that the activity apparently was not only continuing, but was intensifying.

In March of 2005, the recorded history of Father Thomas' computer revealed extensive recent internet activity. The list contained 41 web sites with some of the vilest names imaginable. They were homosexual pornography sites and a majority of them suggested the illegal involvement of teenage boys and younger. I decided that I had to somehow document the list. There is no way to print the list from the keyboard or the menus, so I wrote them down on a sheet of paper. I also knew that at this juncture, I needed to have a witness. I chose to confide in Michael Wilson because I knew him to be a man of impeccable character. Wilson was also employed at the church as Director of Stewardship and Development. I knew Michael loved Father Bill as I did and would never do anything to hurt him. Michael was also a licensed counselor familiar with human behavioral problems and more than experienced with appropriate confidentiality. Michael and I spoke on many occasions in private about the situation and helped each other deal with it.

I did not tell Laura yet. I wanted to protect her. I thought that she would have been mortified to the point of having her faith damaged. Laura was very happy at Holy Cross and really trusted Father Bill. I was unsure how the new lack of trust would have played out in her heart. I was wrong about that and really should have confided in her sooner. She was a lot more capable of dealing with the truth than I gave her credit for.

As time progressed, any sampling of doubt that the nefarious internet activity was actually being personally conducted by Father Thomas vanished. All activity was logged at times when Father was at home, and subsequently, no activity was logged when he was absent.

I knew that it was now imperative that this evidence be documented in some way. It occurred to me while thinking about it, that I could bring the church's digital camera with me the next time I discovered activity. I could photograph the screen with the searches and date/time stamped internet activity revealed and also include enough of the room around the computer monitor to authenticate and validate these photo records. The remainder of the new evidence that I found and as much as I could gather in retrospect was recorded on the digital camera and downloaded onto CDs.

As I was discovering further evidence, it became apparent that Father had become a member of a web site called boycherries.com. According to the internet history on the computer, Father was visiting the site very often. The mastheads on the sub history page listings indicated a welcome to members. Since this site was visited so often, I felt that I had to verify its contents. I was relatively sure that the site, by virtue of its name was pornographic, but thought it was necessary nonetheless to be sure. I opened the site once on my own computer. If you can give the producers of pornography any shred of credit at all it was in the fact that there was a warning index page that initially appeared. On the page there were small photographic vignettes, but they were muted and lacked detail. The purpose of the warning page was apparently for anyone who had arrived there by accident. The site's purpose was verbally detailed in a small boxed paragraph. In the paragraph was the explanation that this was a website to view photos and videos of virginal boys being sexually violated by adult men. There was also an area on the page for members to log in. There was no mistaking now that Father Bill was apparently trapped in the bondage of pornography addiction. And worse, this addiction involved homosexuality with possibly the illegal involvement of children.

"Today there are many CEO's and all too few apostles."
Bishop Fulton Sheen

Chapter Three
Discernment

Father's internet activity continued. The evidence continued to reveal dates and times of site visits that always corresponded with Father's presence in the rectory. I was concerned about Father's apparent addiction and the fact that he was the Catholic clergy representative at the Maxey State Boys Prison, and he was the Diocesan Chaplain for the ministry of Courage and Encourage (ministries endorsed by the Catholic Church to help those experiencing same-sex attraction and their families). It was also very troubling that Father had over fifty altar boys at the time in his service at the parish including my own son. It was also disturbing that Father wanted teenage boys working at the rectory constantly doing odd jobs for him. In light of these mounting concerns, I decided to seek the counsel of Father James Dormond. Father Dormond was the Acting Director of the central offices of Courage and Encourage in New York City. Father Dormond was not only an expert regarding same-sex attraction, but apparently an expert on the significant role the attraction played in the clergy abuse scandal throughout the world. Father was understanding and very helpful. It felt reassuring to have the benefit of his wisdom and direction. We spoke on many occasions and prayed in discernment as to how to deal with this worsening situation at Holy Cross.

I recall really struggling with all of this during one phone call to New York. Father Dormond told me that given that Father Bill is my boss and my employment at the parish is the only means of support for my family, he felt that I would have been able to feel confident before God if I did nothing about this and remained silent. There is no way that this would have been a viable option for me considering all that I had seen. Frankly, I was a bit shocked that Father even suggested it. Oh, make no mistakes, it certainly would have been the easiest route to take. It also would have been the most dangerous. I recall thinking, what if a parish youth is violated? How would I ever forgive myself for being silent? What if the violation occurred and the parents of the youth somehow discovered that I was aware and said nothing? What would have been the moral and ensuing legal implications of that? If silence was an option for Father Dormond and obviously is a favored option for church leadership, it was certainly no option for this husband and father. For the sake of all involved including Father Thomas, disclosure was going to be necessary in some form and at some appropriate time. Obviously confidentiality and prudence would be called for in this disclosure.

Father Dormond told me that considering all aspects of this situation, it was his prediction that if Father Bill had not already moved beyond his pornographic viewing habits and made contact with another person already, statistically, he would at some point. It is certainly curious that Father Dormond would state this just after mentioning silence as an option. I was beginning to question his integrity. Later, as you will see, unfortunately, all this doubt will be substantiated.

During a subsequent discovery at the rectory, I noticed Father visited a link on another pornographic site called, "Meet a Hottie and Hook Up." I was instantly alarmed. This could quite possibly have represented an escalation of Father's addiction and his subsequent attempt to physically meet a young man for illicit purposes. I called Father Dormond. We spoke of now being the time to make preparations to bring the discovery and evidence to the attention of the Diocese of Hamburg and Bishop Martin. Father Dormond was curious and asked about Father Thomas' relationship with Bishop Martin. History has revealed to us that these relationships between leadership and rank and file clergy are apparently quite significant in determining the Church's response to this horrible scandal on local levels.

As an employee of the Church and the Diocese of Hamburg, I was obligated to report any sexual misconduct of any degree to the Moderator of the Curia or the Chancellor of the Diocese, that being Monsignors Michael Mira, and Steven Benke respectively. I decided that I would make an appointment with Monsignor Mira and begin to disclose what I had witnessed under the protective seal of the Sacrament of Confession. Incidentally, Fr. Thomas served his preparatory deaconate prior to his ordination in the late seventies under Mira who was then Pastor of a parish in Brighton, Michigan.

I discussed this method of disclosure with Father Dormond. He agreed that it was a good way to proceed. He also told me that at some point, most likely all hell would break loose at the parish. He certainly did not overestimate this.

During this time our parish was involved in a significant building campaign. There would be a full program to energize the faithful, raise funds and construct a new school and administration build-out. By virtue of my position on the parish staff, I was expected to be a key player in the campaign's administration and ultimate success. I know my deep apprehension was obvious among the top volunteers. They no doubt considered this to be a lack of interest. In reality, I knew that our growth campaign was doomed to failure. I was beholding a healthy effort on behalf of the volunteers to strengthen and grow our parish on one hand while on the other hand coming to terms with the fact that very soon I may have to take action that would quite possibly not only cancel all their efforts but literally shake this faith community to its core.

After many unsuccessful attempts to reach Monsignor Mira, I finally was able to contact him and schedule a Confession. I arrived at the diocesan chancery offices early for the appointment on September 9, 2005. This date just happened to be Laura's and my 23rd wedding anniversary. I sat in the parking lot, shut the car engine off and just prayed. I wished that at that moment, I could be just about any place else in the world.

I revealed my discovery and submitted my evidence to Msgr. Mira under the seal of Confession. Monsignor stated that if he was to do anything at all about this situation, I would have to release him from the sacred confidentiality of the sacrament. I complied. I then made a verbal appeal to him reiterating the written one I had just submitted that I needed my job to be protected by the Diocese. He told me not to worry in the least about that and expressed that I had done the right thing. I felt a sense of peace at these words. I was unaware at that time, however that I had just received a Judas kiss.

I resumed my work at the parish. I was a bit relieved and confident that a difficult part of this ordeal was behind me. I prayed for Father Thomas. I truly believed that when he had to face what he has done, he would humble himself, remove himself from ministry, and seek the proper healing from God and the Church. As long as the youth were protected and no one was yet harmed that we were aware of, this could proceed confidentially. I sympathized with him. I saw him as a victim of his own devices and as a man trapped in the bondage of addiction.

A few days later, the attorney for the Diocese, Mark Kurry called me and asked if he and I could meet that day halfway between the parish and Hamburg. We chose a highway restaurant in Fowlerville. We selected a booth and ordered a couple of soft drinks. Kurry told me that there was once a day when priests who were caught doing things like this would just be reprimanded by their bishops. He told me that those days were gone and allegations of this type had to now be taken very seriously and acted upon swiftly. Of course, we all know about those days when danger signs and real impropriety were virtually ignored. The question seems to be, has anything really changed?

Kurry asked me if my job description and duties afforded me general access to the rectory at the parish. I affirmed that as a business manager, facility manager, and manager of the computer network, I had access to the entire campus. He indicated that was important. Kurry then asked me what my skills were. I asked him why he wanted to know that. He said, "just in case we have to find a different parish for you to work at." I remember thinking, why should I leave? Kurry then suggested we walk outside and continue speaking. I think he was uncomfortable that other patrons in the restaurant may be overhearing our conversation. We went out and walked in the parking lot. Here Kurry told me that Bishop Martin was indeed a shining witness of his office and a true successor of the Apostles. He told me that it would be important for me to now leave this difficult matter in the Bishop's capable hands. He said that I would have to be completely abandoned to his authority in this matter and be satisfied with whatever the Bishop decided. This meeting was somewhat mysterious to me at the time. In retrospect, I believe it was important for diocesan officials to find out just who I was and to attempt to gauge my attitude, intentions and sincerity before they acted in any way. After all, Mr. Kurry was a lawyer. His employer was also his sole client. It is possible that priorities were being set in this early stage of the tragic case, and perhaps this order of priorities had a purpose other than the protection of the innocent.

On September 19, Father was up at his lake house when the Bishop's office contacted him and asked him to come to the Chancery in Hamburg the next morning. Father called me while still up north. He asked me if I knew who was trying to destroy him. He sounded very worried. Of course, I had no idea who was trying to "destroy" him and told him so. If he had asked me if I knew who was trying to help him, I would have had to answer differently. He told me that there was an allegation of internet pornography use against him and that is all diocesan officials would tell him before the meeting. He must have begun the three hour drive back to the parish sometime that evening.

The next morning, about an hour before he had to leave, Father Thomas came into my office. I had never seen him look the way he did that morning. He was withdrawn and deeply troubled. He sank into the chair in front of my desk. He said in a virtual whisper, "who could be doing this to me? " He asserted someone must have gotten into his computer and messed with it. He then suggested it was Anita (Alex's mother). I told him, "if you believe that to be the case, Father, then bring the computer with you to the meeting and give it to the Bishop. They will analyze it and any tampering would most likely be detected." Of course, both Father and I knew the truth that no one had tampered with his computer. Father said, "no, what we really have to do is erase that whole damn thing." I was filled with compassion for Father Thomas that morning. I remember thinking, only a few more hours and he will be safely in the forgiving hands of God and his Bishop and on his way in rectifying his troubled life. I was naïve.

At about 11:30 that morning, Kurry called me at the office. He said that when Father was confronted with the allegation and the evidence, Father told the Bishop that all the pornography on his computer was part of research he was doing on behalf of Courage and Encourage as their regional Chaplain. Well that's strange, Father never mentioned research in my office that morning. He never mentioned research when I brought my initial discovery to his attention thirteen months earlier. He only suggested malicious foul play on the part of others. Why all of a sudden is the explanation completely different now that he is in front of the Bishop? Is it remotely reasonable to even imagine that a priest is conducting research by viewing hours of vile and possibly illegal pornography almost daily for at least fifteen months? Also, in the entire scope of my discovery, not once was any site visited that contained any information that could be considered credible and valid for research. Father Bill never even once visited Courage's own site which contained a wealth of information. Sadly what was unfolding here was the desperate attempt of a man to justify and perhaps mitigate the consequences of an embarrassing and dangerous personal habit.

It was such a tragedy to watch Father Thomas choose the path of obstinacy when the path of humility was not only available to him, but laden with the mercy of God and the protection of his privacy.

Father's false research defense should have been identified as ridiculous by the Bishop. The claim of research has been falsely stressed by so many priests who have been caught with computer pornography in the development of this global crisis. It is simply unacceptable that Bishop Martin was not alerted by this preposterous and pathetic alibi. No one who knows Bishop Martin would believe that he was that stupid. I believe he knew completely what he was dealing with in Father Thomas' addiction and was resolved to respond in the same failed and negligent fashion as so many of his counterparts past and present throughout the world.

Kurry validated my worst fears and said the Bishop seemed to believe Father's story and dismissed the notion that Father was addicted to pornography. Kurry told me that he personally and privately disagreed and believed the truth of Father Thomas' troubling vice as clearly revealed in the evidence. Then, Mr. Kurry told me that the Bishop told Father to go back to the parish, erase all the pornography off the computer and "straighten up and fly right." I was horrified. I hung up the phone, turned off the light, locked my office door, and went home.

"An excuse is worse and more terrible than a lie, for an excuse is a lie guarded ."

Pope John Paul II

Chapter Four
Removal, Accusations, Mystery, and Confusion

The negligence on behalf of Bishop Martin left me completely aghast. To be so flippant regarding this priest considering all the evidence and in the climate that the Church finds itself in today is nothing short of outrageous.

I went back to work the next day. Father Bill was up at the rectory. He called down once or twice to the front office. It was very apparent that he was going to avoid all contact with me. Apparently, in his mind, for all intents and purposes, I was his enemy and betrayer. I remember that Father Dormond had told me that I must see this tragedy as a matter of priorities. First and foremost was the protection of the innocent and the vulnerable. Next was the protection of my livelihood and that of my family (after all, we were also innocent). The next priority was the reputation and credibility of the Church. Last on the priority list was Father Thomas' privacy and reputation.

The next several days were like working around a spoiled, angry child. Father could not bring himself to face me. He was aware I knew the truth. He barked orders through others meant for me. He had the locks changed at the rectory and forbade the maintenance supervisor from sharing the key with me. He even barred me from an important meeting that we had planned for several weeks. His attitude was detestable and it rendered him impossible to work with. He told parishioners that someone close to him had betrayed him and was seeking his destruction, leaving them deeply concerned for him. He told the Chair of the Finance Committee that he was receiving assistance from Mother of God[2] to replace the hard drive of his computer. He told her that someone had hacked into his computer and was depositing data in an effort to bring him down. I found out later that he had told one parishioner, a lawyer named Jude Devlock, that I was indeed this nefarious person who was attacking him. In this willful act of slander, Father had set his sinful plot in motion. He began to build himself a support team that, as time unfolded apparently would stop at nothing to see to it that Father's window-dressed reputation remained unscathed, and his private behavior remained concealed.

Aside from his unacceptable professional conduct at the parish office and its impact on my job, there was something vastly more important and urgent to consider. I knew the truth, that Father was in need of real intervention, and Father knew the truth that he was addicted to youth homosexual pornography. The man remained, however, in a position of access and authority over the young men of the parish. Something had to be done before someone's life was destroyed. Of course, Mr. Kurry at the Diocese also by his own admission knew the truth, but I suppose he considered his job done and obviously, it didn't matter any further. This indifference is consistent with a lawyer-deacon possessing questionable integrity and courage.

I called the ministry head of the altar servers at Holy Cross and asked her to remove my son from the list of Father's servers. As you might expect any decent man to do, I was acting to protect my child. But, what about the other boys? Who was going to protect them? Some of them were the sons of my good friends. And, some of them were strangers. What's the difference when considering their safety? I had thought that my responsibility would be fulfilled when I brought this horrible tragedy to the attention of the Diocese. Obviously it was not finished. I knew in my heart that I was being called to take further action because no one else would.

I was referred to Bob Delisi through a friend. Bob was an attorney in Oakland County. I called him. We discussed what we could possibly do to confront this situation since it certainly seemed no one in church leadership had the courage or even the interest in protecting the innocent. Bob suggested that we needed to go face-to-face with the Bishop. We needed to try to appeal to Bishop Martin to make him understand that he was lied to and that he had a responsibility before God and the Church to act swiftly and surely for the sake of the children and even for Father Bill himself.

I called Monsignor Benke at the Chancery and set an appointment for Delisi and I to meet with the Bishop for the morning of October 4. Meanwhile Mr. Kurry called me just to touch base. I suppose he was interested in how I was handling the news that nothing was going to be done about this. I told him that it was probably not a good idea for us to talk until the meeting. I informed him that I had retained my own legal counsel and was scheduled to see the Bishop. Kurry agreed that we should not speak in the meantime.

A few days later, I was contacted by Special Agent, Robert Peplinski of the Michigan Attorney General's office. He asked me to meet him somewhere away from the parish. I drove to a nearby parking lot to meet him. He interviewed me concerning all aspects of my discovery and asked if I would submit to him a copy of the evidence that I had gathered. I handed the envelope and the CD containing the internet history of Father Bill's computer to Peplinski. I had previously made several copies of the evidence to be able to have it with me and at the same time have the originals safely in storage.

On the morning of October 4, I met Bob Delisi at a restaurant in Howell. I got into his car and we drove together to Hamburg. Assembled in the room for the meeting was Bishop Martin, Monsignor Mira, Mr. Kurry, Delisi and myself. I started the meeting by reading this multi page statement that I had prepared:

DIOCESAN MEETING Tuesday, October 4, 2005

The diocesan program to address the clergy sex abuse scandal is called "Protecting God's Children." By the decision to retain Father Thomas in active ministry, the church is failing to protect God's children. Father Thomas has 47 altar boys. He is the diocesan chaplain for the Courage/Encourage Program (A national ministry to, believe it or not, teach chastity and holiness to homosexuals in an effort to bring them back to the Church and the Sacraments).

During the time that I was gathering the evidence and discovering Father Bill's internet activity, I was also being as diligent as I could be in keeping a watchful eye on Father and the male teens of the parish. This past spring, Father mentioned to me that he needed a teenage boy to be up at the rectory employed by the church to do odd jobs. I recall thinking that I will never permit this. If Father persisted I knew I was going to have to tell him at some point, no, there will be no boy at the rectory. Father did mention it a few more times but then stopped asking.

The youth room is in the basement of the rectory. There on several nights a month, teens gather for fun and fellowship. Father also has access to the boys incarcerated at the Maxey Boys prison as the Catholic Chaplain. He hears their confessions and counsels them privately. If he ever touches one of them and the State of Michigan discovers it, they would literally and publicly crucify Father and the Catholic Church.

I hoped and believed that when the time was right and this was brought before the church that Father would humble himself. I hoped and believed that he would remove himself from ministry and seek healing and reconciliation with God. When confronted by the bishop with visual evidence from Father's computer, Father did not humble himself and submit to church leadership and action. Rather, Father lied and told the Bishop this was research for his leadership role in the Courage and Encourage Ministry. In all of my personal investigation of Father's internet activity never once has a site been visited that provided any information that could be considered research. Never once was there any sites visited that seemed to provide insight either medical or otherwise pertaining to same sex attraction. Never once had Courage's own web site which provides much related information been visited. What was visited? Nothing but reprehensible pornography. Hours and hours spent in front of images that bring delight only to deviant sex addicts. The national assistant leader of Courage/Encourage, Father Dormond in New York was outraged that Father would use their work as an excuse for his disordered compulsion. They exclaimed that NEVER is anyone to conduct research about the homosexual condition by utilizing internet pornography. According to what I was told, Bishop Martin apparently believed that father was conducting research. I understand he then told Father to clean his computer and "straighten up and fly right."

Father's denial and his subsequent childish behavior toward me has completely changed this entire situation and elevated it to a seriously high level status of alert. I believe with all my heart that the young men of Holy Cross Parish are not safe while Father is serving in ministry there. Statistical criteria from Courage and Encourage states that he will act on his passions if he has not already. Father Dormond was also further alarmed when I relayed to him that Father Bill has been of late verbally minimizing sins of the flesh. And, Father Bill also told me in private conversation that he feels consensual sex with minors is no where near as grave a situation as forced molestation. Needless to say this was just as alarming to Father Dormond by illustrating Father's growing rationalization of his behavior.

Boycherries.com is the site that was a particular favorite of Father's. The evidence shows that he has spent countless hours viewing pornographic videos and photos of teen boys being violated by grown men for the first time.

Father has apparently begun to seek out contact with others who share his compulsion. There is evidence that a link was visited entitled: "Meet a Hottie and hook-up" One of Father's last efforts was according to visual evidence a joining of a site called: "Hookedonteens.com." This evidence is grave and renders Father unfit for contact with young men.

The Policy and Procedures Manual for Sexual Misconduct published by the Diocese of Hamburg is very clear that I was compelled to bring the evidence of Father's deeds to the attention of diocesan leadership.

When Father Bill knew he was being called to Hamburg but before he appeared, he sat before me and deeply wondered who was trying to destroy him by getting into his computer. Curiously, no mention was made to me of the extensive homosexual research he had been conducting either at this time or the time last September when I made him aware of what I first discovered on his computer. I suggested that Father Bill bring his computer to the Bishop at the meeting and hand it over to them to have its hard drive analyzed. This would reveal any tampering. Father, of course did not consider this to be a good idea. He said "what we really need to do is erase all the crap off of it." Apparently the diocesan leadership agreed with Father and asked him to "clean" the computer. I do not understand how the diocese could even suggest this legally dangerous move of erasing the computer in light of what the church has been undergoing for the past several years regarding the homosexual misbehavior of clergy.

The diocese tells me that I did the right thing. They say my job is protected. However, I am paying a high price for this "protection". Father is blatantly ignoring me. He has not shared one single word with me since his secret was exposed. He barks commands to me through the office staff. He is banning me from meetings at which I was scheduled to appear. He has changed the locks in the rectory and has forbidden my access to the new keys. He is gathering a group around him and telling them that someone close to him has betrayed him. People then call me for more information about this supposedly evil man who is trying to destroy Father. My rights in the workplace are in jeopardy due to Father's behavior. My honor, position and good name in the parish are being threatened by this shocking and childish display.

Father displays an inordinate amount of attention to certain teenage boys. (Never to girls or women). Father actually had Alex Sanchez spending a considerable amount of time at the rectory. He gave Alex a key to the house, a cell phone (paid for by the parish) and access to his computer/internet. He would take Alex to ball games, out to eat and shop on many occasions. He also had Alex on the payroll as a part-time employee before the boy's mother unexpectedly and emphatically severed the relationship. Alex simply disappeared. Other young men catch Father's eye from time to time and he does not even realize how obvious he becomes when he shows this interest.

Father Bill is steeped in his own sin. I believe he has lost all grace and wisdom. I believe anyone would whom rather than accepting responsibility for their sin will deny their sin and make up lies to cover it. He apparently will even attempt to destroy my good name in an effort to cover his shameful acts.

I have had to remove my son from the altar serving program and could not tell him why. He thinks he is being punished for something. 46 other boys remain on the program. Many of them are sons of my dear friends. I will not leave them vulnerable to Father's sin. I have had to remove my other children from Father's Apologetics class. I do not want him in a situation of influence over any of my children.

Apparently, the Diocese of Hamburg is giving Father Bill the benefit of the doubt. I have no such doubts. I watched all of the dynamics of this dreadful situation unfold. I know what is happening and what is at stake. Can the diocese afford to be wrong on any of this?

I am being asked to work under a man who truly hates me and will work against me at every chance. Besides I know that he is a

41

real threat to the youth of our parish. He must be removed permanently from contact with youngsters.

Why should I have to suffer for doing the right thing? Do we wonder why people do not come forward to expose wrongdoing when you consider the consequences? Why should they?

There are two options for us to move on from here.

Option one: Father is at the age of retirement. He must be sent into immediate retirement free from contact with teens. I am insisting that notice of his immediate retirement reach me before Wednesday, October 5 midnight. If this happens, I will remain silent because proper, holy and prudent action will have been undertaken to protect the faithful. I beg you to choose this option.

Option two: The Diocese chooses the status quo. I will know whether or not this option has been chosen by Thursday morning. If it has, I will immediately inform the parish of my investigation and discovery. I will do this because to fail to do it would be a gravely immoral sin of omission. If I am fired for this action or any retaliation is inflicted upon me, I will have no choice but to seek legal action against the Diocese and Father personally.

I don't want option two to be the choice. This would damage my children's faith and the faith of many at Holy Cross. Someone will be held accountable before God for this damage and it's not going to be me.

Furthermore, it is most unfortunate and very disappointing that the lack of response to Father's offenses and his resulting spoiled brat reaction have necessitated that I address you here today. The strongly perceived threat to my rights has compelled me to retain legal counsel. Because this should have been unnecessary, I am insisting that the Diocese of Hamburg reimburse me for my legal expenses to date.

Patrick J. Flynn

I became emotional momentarily when I reached the part where I had to remove my son from the list of servers. Bob asked the Bishop a single question. He asked, "can you afford to be wrong about this, Bishop?" We also discussed that I had already met with

42

the Attorney General's agent and that I had given the evidence to him. The Bishop became quite curious when he learned that law enforcement was actively investigating the matter. He must not have known yet that they had been contacted. I did not contact the authorities. I came to find out from the police report once it was released that Mr. Kurry had contacted the Livingston County Prosecutor's office and reported the incident. The Bishop said, "We know now what we have to do."

It was somewhat of a relief to have the indication that action would be taken. The meeting was adjourned. As I was leaving, Mr. Kurry turned to me and said, "You're a good man." Amazing. Even Jesus Christ himself was not kissed by Judas twice.

Father was handed a letter from the Bishop the next day. The letter told him that he must leave the parish immediately and go up to his lake house. He was further instructed by Bishop Martin to only offer the Mass privately in his residence, to leave all keys, and other parish property behind, especially his desktop and laptop computers.

Once again Father Thomas was being given an opportunity to do the right thing. He could have humbled himself, admitted what had transpired and sought the help he so desperately needed without the need for any further disclosure. Once again, this would not happen. As he was leaving, Father apparently called three men up to the rectory and told them that I was framing him. Sean Lovard, the parish's Director of Religious Education was one of those summoned. These gentlemen confided to me personally the details of this meeting. Father told them that I was insane and his removal was an injustice. Interestingly before he left, he made a startling confession to the men. He told them what he did was immoral, but not illegal. This was a strange admission. A priest describes his supposed research as immoral? And, what of the hacker story? This was all supposed to be the work of a mysterious phantom with ill intentions conspiring with me. How sadly pathetic.

That evening Father Thomas was gone from the parish. His absence, however, was only physical. Father Thomas still would retain his title of Pastor and indefinitely receive his full pay and benefits. He continually sought contact with various parishioners as a deeply sinful plan to personally destroy my career and personal character began to take form.

Father did not head up to his lake house as Bishop Martin had ordered. He instead spent several days at the home of parishioner and attorney Jude Devlock in Brighton a few miles from the church.

Devlock was indeed the right man to conduct and manage a campaign to cover up the truth regarding Father Thomas and vilify the whistleblower. Apparently no tools would be off the table in waging this campaign including lies, bullying, deception, slander, libel. It did not seem to matter that those involved were self-confessed Christians and their chosen tools were mortally sinful. But, Father's character had already been sadly established and the characters of those who vowed to help him would soon reveal varying and troubled levels of personal corruption.

The malicious intent of Father's supporters coupled with his slandering of me upon his departure fertilized the soil for rampant gossip, confusion, and mystery concerning this now suddenly missing leader.

The next morning, Sean Lovard met me in the parking lot when I arrived for work. He was visibly upset and wanted some answers in light of the events of the previous evening. I was reminded once again that the path of humility is a scarcely travelled road for Father Bill Thomas. I asked Sean to be patient until I could get into my office and speak to my attorney. I wanted to address this properly, especially at this volatile stage. I reached Delisi at his office. Although somewhat incredible, if you work for the church in 2005, apparently it's a really good idea to maintain your own legal counsel on retainer. I told Bob that apparently Father did not leave quietly, but falsely and maliciously implicated me to several people before vacating the rectory the night before. Delisi told me, under the circumstances, to assemble whatever staff was present and tell them the truth as to what went down.

I was able to gather Sean, the parish secretary, the receptionist, the bookkeeper and the bookstore manager in Sean's office. They were obviously devastated to hear the truth about Father. They did seem to believe the facts and accept that I was telling them the truth. After all, they worked with Father and all of them knew that something had been very wrong for a very long time in both his personal and priestly life. Our youth director, a young woman in her twenties, was not in the office that morning. She arrived for work that afternoon, came directly into my office, closed the door and began to sob. She told me through her tears that she had just heard that Father was taken away for sexual misconduct. She immediately expressed deep concerns that perhaps one of the parish youth under her care had fallen victim in some way. I assured her that was not the case as far as we knew. I told her that if history proved us lucky, the action taken against Father was pre-emptive and perhaps not a moment too soon.

I told the remainder of the staff all of the facts as soon as I could. I spoke separately to our music director, the RCIA director, the maintenance director and the Deacon, Jack Boehman. Boehman was only with the church for about a month. He didn't know Father Thomas very well nor did he know me very well either. I sensed from the very first few minutes of our meeting, that Boehman was not going to accept the truth concerning this tragedy. This denial on his part would prove to be a very serious problem in the many months to come as the Deacon would soon join the small group of Father's supporters and begin to help them with their agenda to silence the truth and exhibit open contempt for me. This was especially problematic due to the fact that he was a member of the clergy and worked on assignment from the Diocese. Unfortunately, Boehman would come to be only one of many clergy and church officials who refuse to do the right thing.

On October 7, Father David Douelle, the Judicial Vicar of our region of the Diocese came to address the staff. Here was another opportunity for those in authority to do the right thing - another opportunity sadly missed. Father Douelle told the staff to tell everyone that Father Thomas *voluntarily* took a leave of absence for personal reasons, and that we would be sent a temporary priest to take his place. Of course what Father Douelle was telling us to do was wrong. It simply wasn't true. I remember thinking how can we adequately address a crisis when truth is avoided at the very onset? There was no way that I was going to tell people that Father Bill left by his own choice especially after he slandered me upon his departure. I discovered some time later from Mr. Kurry that the Diocese never told Father Douelle to say that about Father Bill's departure. Or did they? Who knows? This whole drama was beginning to smell a bit like a cover up. Apparently I was not learning my lesson concerning naivete. I was still confident that this crisis would be appropriately handled by church officials if for no other reason than to avoid the media fire storm that would ensue.

In the days that followed, parishioners wondered, mystery ruled the day, people surmised different scenarios, rumors began to spread and Father's apologists rolled up their sleeves and went to work with their agenda, at the same time refusing to objectively observe the evidence all around them.

Rumors began to make their way full circle. An outspoken woman in the parish was diverting inquiring parishioners from me and directing them to Jude Devlock for "clarification." Teresa Panky was determined to defend Father Thomas by whatever means necessary. She and her husband actually moved 50 miles from Dearborn to be near Father and become members of his parish. Teresa was obviously burdened with some internal issues of her own. She could not seem to control her emotions and ended up isolating herself from many in the parish since her arrival. She was, however, aggressive and unrelenting. It makes sense and would become quite obvious in this case that people who are struggling with their own demons will not be able to handle the truth when an idol of their own creation is shown to be anything less than who they imagined him to be.

On October 7, 2005, Father Steve Klanyi arrived as our temporary Canonical Administrator. Father immediately informed us that he was told nothing about our situation and wanted it to stay that way. He said he wanted to truthfully say he did not know when people asked him what had happened, which they were sure to do. It is reasonable to assume that Father Klanyi was a lot less ignorant of the situation than he was revealing. There wasn't a priest in the Diocese who did not find out what was going on when one of them is suddenly removed from ministry. In reality, time would prove that the Diocese could not really have sent a worse man for the job than Klanyi. Or was he perhaps the best man for them to send regarding the current state of church leadership and the rotten plots and putrid hearts of guilty men?

A short while after Klanyi's arrival, I was told by friends who knew the man that Klanyi was the worst possible choice the Bishop could have sent to a parish undergoing such a crisis. They predicted that Father would do absolutely nothing to control the situation nor bring healing based on his poor leadership in other parishes. I remember thinking that if they are right, we are going to be in for one hell of a ride.

Since 2001, the parish contracted the help of a priest to come and offer one of our Masses every Sunday. Father Michael Pride was employed at the Mother of God School of Law as their Chaplain. Having no parish of his own to offer the Mass, he assisted at Holy Cross. Realizing the Diocese was not attending to the spiritual needs of the parish or Father Bill, Laura and I perceived that perhaps Father Pride would help in this regard.

After one of the Sunday Masses in early November, I approached Father Pride in the corridor as he was leaving. I was reaching out to him regarding the spiritual needs for our parish and Father Bill. He cut me short and railed against me. He bellowed within earshot of several parishioners, "Did you know fifty percent of men in the confessional struggle with pornography?" He then stormed off. He was about as rude and arrogant as anyone could be, priest or otherwise. His refusal to deal with the truth of what occurred prompted me to write the following letter:

November 28, 2005

Fr. Michael Pride
Mother of God School of Law

Dear Fr. Pride,

I attempted to approach you in the hallway at church a few weeks ago. I had a concern regarding Fr. Thomas' removal from the parish and thought that you could assist me. It was quite apparent that you did not wish to discuss the matter and obviously, your mind was made up to support Fr. Thomas unreservedly.

It has now come to my attention that a parishioner has discussed this topic with you and now is of the mind that I am quite the culprit in this situation.

Father, with all due respect you don't seem to care enough to hear the truth about Father's removal so I feel it is necessary to enlighten you.

Father Thomas' removal is not the result of a misunderstanding on any level. Father has been steeped in the dark sin of teenage homosexual internet pornography for some time. Father claims that research on his computer is being used to bring him down. What an outrage! In the year and a half of my findings, never once had any website been visited that would have contained any research. Courage and Encourage has a website that is packed with research on homosexuality. Father was their Diocesan Chaplain. He never even visited their site once. Father made himself a member of Boycherries.com, a website that caters to the fetish of watching virginal boys being violated by grown men. Is this research? Hours and hours, day after day, months on end entertaining oneself with this reprehensible material?

I have included with this letter, a Chronology of Discovery that I presented to the Diocese when I reported this. Bear in mind this was before Father went into his shameful denial. I truly believed that when presented with the evidence by his bishop, Father would have humbled himself and begin the process of repentance. I was very wrong in assuming he would do that. Refer to the Chronology. This was no one-time incident nor was it "misunderstood pastoral research" of any kind. Father knows this and subsequently lied to Bishop Martin.

48

In lamenting his situation and attempting to garner support, Father told a parishioner that he was going to bring his computer to Mother of God and have the hard drive wiped out. If his computer contained valid research, then its hard drive was Father's best defense. I'm not stupid Father, and neither are you. Father Thomas apparently attempted to destroy the evidence of his sin. When the State Police seized the computer, it had already been compromised. The destroying of evidence in a case like this can be very serious. The criminal investigation is ongoing as we speak.

I'm guessing that Father Thomas failed to mention to you that I originally approached him personally and revealed my findings on his computer. He denied any knowledge of the content that lay before him directly on his own computer screen. He suggested foul play and tampering of his computer by others. Curiously, Father did not claim that the content at that time was research. That's because it wasn't.

Father has slandered me since his removal. He is holding audience with many parishioners and is arrogantly professing his innocence. He is lying and he knows it. Shame on him and God help him.

Father, I don't expect you to come to me wanting to see the evidence I have photographed over the year and a half that I have been monitoring Father's internet activity. But the evidence is there and it reveals a very tragic and disturbing double-life of a Catholic priest. I realize that the crisis that the Church is enduring has had its share of false accusations and thirty-year-old allegations. This is neither. I know exactly what it was that I discovered and reported to the Diocese.

I realize that prior to this correspondence your only source of information was from Father Thomas. But, then again, you did not seek any information from me or the church staff. I will ask one thing of you if I may. If you have been active in maligning my good name in this parish, I am asking you to stop that now please. If you have been actively defending Father with limited information, I would also ask you to please reconsider that.

I am sorry for the blunt tone of this letter, but in all fairness, Father, you set the mood for that in our last meeting.

May God bless you and help you to understand what has happened.

Most sincerely,

Patrick Flynn
Business Manager
Holy Cross Roman Catholic Church

Father Pride had made up his mind and joined Father Thomas in his denial. This would be an all too familiar scenario regarding many clergy and their failure to even acknowledge the sex abuse scandal. I was at the time unaware that Fr. Pride's affections overwhelmingly sided with the predators and built a system of contempt for victims. Below in Pride's own words we see his desire for increased protection for predators and perpetrators through the bolstering of cover up:

"Priests' Privacy and Reputation Need Protection"
by (Rev.) Michael P. Pride, Ed.D.

The recent state of priest sex abuse scandals and the willingness of some bishops to turn over clergy files to law enforcement agencies should move priests to be proactive in periodically reviewing what their personnel files contain. This is an especially pressing matter if a recent settlement involving the Diocese of Manchester, New Hampshire, which allows the state to review priests' records for five years, is copied in other jurisdictions. Sadly, carelessly kept or ambiguous notes, dubious letters, errant recollections, unsubstantiated allegations, privileged priest-bishop conversations and other confidential information have caused harm to the reputation of clergy both living and dead. And, because the dead cannot defend themselves, the tarnishing of their legacy has caused unmitigated pain to their families, friends, and past parishioners.

A priest should never release to a bishop his full psychological or medical reports. A summary evaluation of the priest's ability or inability to return to some form of ministry is all that is necessary. A full report may be misconstrued and allow more information than is necessary or helpful for the good of the priest and the untrained eyes of chancery officials. It is also important to reiterate that this "client-professional" privileged information may find its way into discovery.

50

The events of the past years' scandals – the numerous civil and criminal suits brought against bishops for negligence and clergy for pedophilia and statutory rape – have made renewed caution in clergy recordkeeping vitally important. Aside from the legal issues, this crisis is also an opportunity for bishops to reconsider and refine the recordkeeping on their clergy. It's not only consistent with our belief in the dignity of the person and his right to privacy and reputation, but it is good business practice.

For Father Pride, however, the involvement in this particular cover up concerning Fr. Thomas was more substantial than his arrogant philosophical denial of the scandal.

During the weeks that followed, I received a call from Joe Kelly, one of the Deans of the law school. He had heard that the institution may have been involved in the tampering of evidence and was inquiring if I knew any more about this. I told Dean Kelly that I only knew what the Chair of the Finance Committee relayed to me following her conversation with Father Thomas regarding Mother of God to erase his computer. The Dean was understandably upset and made reference to the fact that the school could suffer greatly if this indeed were true. Based upon my knowledge, I simply could not confirm or deny the school's involvement at the time.

An unnamed source, an employee at the Mother of God School of Law would eventually reveal that Father Pride was actually involved in the tampering of evidence and ensuing silence regarding what would be revealed as the actual replacement of the offending computer's hard drive. Pride helped Father Bill by directing him to the IT department of the Mother of God School of Law. There Father Bill was able with their help and the help of others to remove the hard drive from his computer and replace it with a brand new one in the days before his removal from the parish. Pride would eventually admit his shameful involvement in this scandal under pressure. Although apparently Dean Kelly was unaware, the IT Department, Father Pride, Dean Forski, and possibly Phil Domino knew of the school's involvement in helping

Father Bill manipulate evidence. They helped him in the midst of a criminal investigation by the Michigan State Police and Attorney General. Shamefully, silence and obstruction were the rules of the day with these "catholic" men who seemed to never shy from the spotlight to boast of their principled and holy leadership.

"A failure to speak the truth because of a misconceived sense of compassion should not be taken for love. We do not have the right to minimize matters of our own accord, even with the best of intentions. Our task is to be God's witnesses, to be spokesmen of a mercy that saves even when it shows itself as JUDGMENT on man's sin."

Pope John Paul II, *2002. (emphasis his)*

Chapter Five
The Anatomy of Denial.

This chapter is tangential yet relevant at this point.

Facts are. To exist, facts do not require us to believe. Fact, whether accepted or rejected, remains mere fact. Reality is neither affected by consensus nor by objective or subjective perception. I can look at the sun and then proclaim and even convince myself that it is neither hot nor bright. That has absolutely no effect on reality because the fact remains that the sun is both hot and bright. I can create the fantasy that it is cool and dim and even persuade you to agree with me, but what have I changed? Did I change the characteristics of the sun with my rejection of objective truth?

In our story's tragic drama, there is initially, a pattern of misbehavior. I discovered, studied, and chronicled this misbehavior. At a point in my observations, I knew that the behavior was fact and not merely suspicion because I actually watched it unfold over the span of fifteen months and document itself in Father Thomas' computer. But in all fairness, others would not be able to know for sure that the activity was factual until they beheld real evidence. Real evidence for others that the misbehavior was now indisputable fact came when the Michigan State Police discovered the whereabouts of Father Thomas' original drive, verified the contents and documented the evidence in the official report of their investigation.

In virtually every parish where a priest was removed for impropriety, there will emerge a group of people determined to support the priest by professing his innocence at all costs and despite all evidence. They convince themselves and others to reject indisputable fact. As in the example of the sun above, they have not changed reality. Fact is not all of a sudden fiction by virtue of their rejection. That is because once again, facts simply are. These people actively deceive themselves and in turn cause great harm to their parish and community. This phenomenon is explored in Chapter Sixteen.

The question is why would otherwise intelligent people attempt to identify fact as fiction? Why would they try to accomplish the impossible? In this case and all other cases of its kind, the rejection of fact is necessary to alter their psychological version of the event. We see this play out in other venues as well, such as spousal and child abuse and also in cults. In rejecting fact, these individuals can then cling to their psychologically manufactured version of the event and securely believe this virtual alteration rather than the painful actual truth. This now becomes their "reality" which differs greatly from factual reality. This is virtually always the result of individual psychological dynamics, for better or for worse. We have all observed cases whereas family members of an accused perpetrator are absolutely convinced of his or her innocence. In this example it is the familial bond that is so strong as to affect sound, objective reason. Further complicating such situations is the fact that the perpetrator lies to family and friends and denies the misbehavior. Those close to the accused have a very strong desire and predisposition to accept the concept of innocence.

We create our own icons and idols. This has intrigued behavioral scientists for centuries. We tend to build up in other human beings that which either is lacking in ourselves or in those we were supposed to have been able to trust. Therefore, when we "iconize" another human being, asking us to accept factual reality regarding less than iconic behavior in them is simply out of the question. Subconsciously this could be the fear that if good things are proven to be bad, then perhaps there is no good. It is a phobia, a psychological aberration of sort.

If the aggressive individuals in this story were to accept the documented fact that Father Thomas is addicted to post-adolescent homosexual pornography, the disappointment would perhaps be too much to endure. Perhaps they fear that they could never forgive him. Perhaps this has a connection to others in their lives, maybe even themselves. Consequently, there is no shortage of excuses for rejecting uncomfortable facts. They are varied and quite problematic.

Chapter Six
State Police and Attorney General Investigations

On October 17, 2005, I was contacted in my office by Detective Sean Furlong of the Michigan State Police. Detective Furlong informed me that the State Police now had jurisdiction over the investigation ending the active involvement of both the Attorney General and the County Prosecutor. The detective told me that he wanted to come to the parish. He asked me if I would accompany him to the rectory and turn on Father Bill's computer in his presence. He arrived about an hour later. I walked with him up to the rectory. I told him that I had not been in the rectory since before bringing my evidence to the Diocese. When we arrived in the rectory study, I noticed Father Bill's computer was sitting in the middle of the floor, completely disconnected. This would reasonably indicate that the computer had been transported somewhere and placed back in the rectory. Furlong asked if I would connect the computer to its monitor and power it up. I did as he had asked. During the boot-up process, the monitor remained blank. The detective indicated that apparently the computer was tampered as the Windows operating system would not even launch. Of course, since Bishop Martin mishandled this situation, Father Bill had two weeks between the time of the first meeting and his departure to do whatever he pleased with the computer. It was during this interval that the computer was handled by the law school. Furlong told me that he was going to get the proper credentials to seize the computer. He returned later that day. After getting a signature of release from Father Klanyi, I put both the desktop computer and Father Bill's laptop computer into the trunk of Furlong's car as he had instructed.

On October 26, Jude Devlock called me at my office. We had scheduled a sub-committee meeting of some parish leaders for that evening. It had become necessary to reveal the truth to key people due to the rumors and confusion. Devlock armed with ulterior motives, wanted to know if he could come into my office early and view the evidence that I had recorded on the CD. He arrived about 5 pm. I was not aware at the time that Father Thomas had already engaged Devlock in crafting a cover up. Devlock pretended that he was objective and still my friend. Neither was true. Devlock viewed the contents of the CD and told me he believed it was substantial as evidence. I told him that the police had just recently seized Father's computer and were analyzing the hard drive as we speak. He didn't seem to flinch at this news.

The meeting went off as planned at 6:30 that evening. When I began to divulge what I discovered, both Devlock and Parish Council President, Mike Drenski shut me down. They said they would not hear these things about Father without him being present to defend himself. Strange, but I don't recall being present to defend the truth or myself during the three days that Father Bill spent at Devlock's residence crafting his alibi and assassinating my character. Allowing Devlock and Drenski to silence the truth that evening was a grave mistake. After all, discovering and coming to terms with the truth was supposed to be the sheer purpose of the meeting.

A few days later, detective Furlong called me. He said that the hard drive on Father Thomas' computer had apparently been scrubbed of all data. There didn't seem to be anything else they could do. I called Devlock with this latest development. He seemed satisfied. He knew the truth, however, that the police were looking at the wrong drive and yet he remained silent, content that Father possibly could evade any accountability. As you will see, the police investigation would later reveal that the drive they were analyzing was brand new, and that Devlock himself was actually in possession of the original drive that was removed at the law school. It is no less than appalling that this man, who is an attorney and a supposed Christian had the gall to conceal evidence during a criminal investigation thereby placing the boys of the parish in possible danger.

On November 10 according to State Police records, a meeting was held at the Diocese. Jude Devlock accompanied Father Thomas to this meeting. The Diocese learned at this meeting that Devlock was in possession of the original computer hard drive and had kept the location of this vital evidence from authorities for more than five weeks. The Diocese subsequently called the State Police to report this. Detective Furlong immediately sought a search warrant to retrieve the drive. On November 18, Livingston County Judge Teresa Brennan issued the warrants for both Devlock's office and residence. When Furlong and a State Trooper showed up at Devlock's door, he then, mentally processing the trouble he faced, surrendered the drive.

The investigation now continued with the actual hard drive that was in Father Thomas' computer during the entire discovery period. The drive was taken to the Michigan State Police computer crime lab and its contents analyzed. Evidence of youth related gay male searches, a fair amount of adult gay pornographic images, evidence of Father's membership and passwords to three pornographic web sites, and seven images of possible child pornography were discovered by State Police authorities.

Although the discovery was horrifyingly inappropriate to be found on any man's computer, most especially that of a priest, the only material that could have been considered illegal were the seven images of possible child pornography. According to the police report, these images were discovered in the unallocated portion of the drive. This is where files end up that are placed in the recycle bin and then dumped from the bin. They are therefore missing certain digital data necessary to prosecute under Michigan law. Once again, due to the fact that Bishop Martin failed to act appropriately at the initial meeting with Father Thomas, ample time was provided permitting the tampering of evidence. Additionally, Father's membership to the web sites could have been illegal if the sites, in fact used minors in their production. The police decided, for whatever reason to look no further into this due to the fact that membership was necessary to navigate the sites in question and investigate further. As mentioned previously, the site, boycherries.com claims to show virginal minor boys being violated by grown men. Another site that Father joined as a member was twinks.com. The word, twink is a homosexual slang term meaning a "cute young thing." It is perplexing as to why the State Police would not try to establish the legal status of these sites considering their titles and inference. They had a public duty to thoroughly investigate this for the benefit of public safety and did not.

In the beginning of December, I sent an email to Mr. Kurry. In the correspondence, I told him that I would have to begin telling the full truth about Father Thomas. The level and intensity of the rumors and misinformation had been permitted to run rampant due to the silence of those in authority. Kurry called me and asked me if I would come down to the Diocese and discuss this. We set an appointment. I brought Laura with me. In the meeting, despite our best efforts to convince them that the truth was necessary, Mr. Kurry and Monsignor Mira insisted that we and they remain silent. I knew in my heart that the truth and only the truth was called for at this point. These men held sway over my family's livelihood. Their decision to withhold necessary information from the faithful was pure scandal but they were tying my hands to do the right thing unilaterally. I did tell them that I would, however, tell the truth when the circulating rumors cast doubt or suspicion concerning my character and personal honor. I reminded them that I have every canonical, civil, and moral right to defend my family against calumny.

In the same meeting, besides pleading for spiritual assistance for Father Thomas, Laura and I asked Monsignor to please in the very least have Bishop Martin or one of his representatives come to the parish to address our people. We tried to make them understand the value of showing the faithful they at least cared about them, loved them and were committed to seeing them through this catastrophe. Mira refused. He said although we may not understand, to say nothing is best. He expressed that in his experience, it is frustrating to field questions by the faithful that cannot legally be answered. Their plan of action was silence, the patently unholy choice of weak men, and the historically proven fertile soil for the cultivation of harm and scandal.

On January 9, Mr. Kurry called me to tell me that the State Police informed him that the investigation would be closed soon and the report would become public information. Kurry wanted me to understand that the Diocese did not want this report distributed.

This is in direct violation of the Diocese' own published policy of open, and truthful disclosure.

> "In cases of alleged sexual misconduct, it is important that accurate information be shared with the media. The level of disclosure must always be balanced against the concern for privacy and the rights of the victim as well as the accused. Prompt disclosure of information will help dispel the atmosphere of distrust and misinformation that may be fed by rumors."
>
> *Sexual Misconduct Policy and Procedures, p.7*
> *Roman Catholic Diocese of [Hamburg]*

This policy was reviewed and approved by Kurry himself prior to its publishing. Once again, silence is sought as a means of avoiding full accountability of this tragedy.

The investigation was closed on January 23, 2006. There would be no formal criminal charges against Father Thomas, however, the troubling full report of the investigation would be sent to the Diocese of Hamburg and then made available to the public via the Freedom of Information Act. Father's supporters in the parish were filled with glee that there would be no charges. They, led by Devlock would begin deceptively marketing this news as Father's complete exoneration. Exoneration is defined as having all guilt removed. The spin that Devlock would put on this was designed to have people believe just that. Truth be told, being addicted to homosexual pornography and enjoying it continuously is not illegal, but it's a far cry from innocence, especially so for a priest with considerable access to the young males of the parish.

"And he came up to Him to Kiss Him. And when he had come, he went right up to Him and said, 'Rabbi, hail, Rabbi.' And he kissed Him." In this same way Christ is approached, greeted, called *"Rabbi,"* kissed, by those who pretend to be Disciples of Christ, professing His teaching in name but striving in fact to undermine it by crafty tricks. . . . In just this way is He kissed by those priests who consecrate the most holy body of Christ and then put to death Christ's members, Christian souls, by their false teaching and wicked example. *"*

St. Thomas More, The Sadness of Christ

Chapter Seven
The Spin Begins

Father Thomas was not going to face criminal charges. This news was seized upon by Devlock and Father's supporters.

There is a propensity to believe that if someone is not convicted of a crime, they are innocent of all wrongful behavior. The constitutional tenet of presumed innocence until proven otherwise is indeed a necessary maxim for a free society's structure of civil law. We are very fortunate to have such a constitutional principle for our protection. But, civil law and moral behavior are certainly not mutually consistent. For example, if I were to take a mistress, waste my family's resources on excessive gambling and drinking, I indeed have committed no crimes even if there is documented proof of my actions. I will neither be charged nor convicted before a judge, magistrate or jury. But the fact is that I am guilty of these sins nonetheless. If I or my friends claim that I am innocent by virtue of the non-existent legal charges, we would all be mistaken.

In January of 2006, Jude Devlock wrote and faxed a document to the parish and convinced a member of the Parish Council to distribute it that evening at the Council meeting. In this document, the following false statements were made:

> The origin of the youth homosexual material and web site traffic on Fr. Thomas' computer is a matter of dispute.
>
> There were no pornographic images found on the computer.
>
> Fr. Thomas wanted to be interviewed by the State Police.
>
> Fr. Thomas had not slandered the whistleblower in this case.
>
> Fr. Thomas did not tamper with evidence in this case.
>
> I (Devlock) obtained the hard drive from Fr. Thomas' computer and quickly surrendered it to the State Police to prove his innocence.

The ministries of Courage / Encourage were remaining neutral involving testimony against Fr. Thomas, one of their Regional Chaplains.

The official Michigan State Police report would ultimately not only expose Devlock as a liar, but document his actual involvement in obstruction and cover up.

On January 10, two weeks before the police investigation was even concluded, a meeting was held and attended by at least twenty two of Father Thomas' sympathizers. The meeting apparently took place at Devlock's home in Hartland. Obviously a strategy was discussed among them as to how to spin the facts enough to get Father Thomas back to the parish. They decided to draft a formal letter to Bishop Martin demanding Father's return. The letter draws false and dangerous conclusions, and attempts to malign my character and cast my intentions into suspicion. The text of the letter follows:

> January 10. 2006 - Feast Day of St. William of Bourges Patron Saint of Ecclesiastical Rights
>
> The Most Reverend Carl F. Martin
> Bishop of Hamburg
>
> Subject: Support for our Pastor at Holy Cross Parish, Father Wesley Thomas
>
> Your Excellency:
>
> We, the undersigned, are prominent and active leaders and parishioners at Holy Cross Parish in Hamburg. As you are aware, our pastor, Father Wesley Thomas, has been on temporary leave of absence since October 6, 2005. We respectfully and charitably understand that the Diocese has maintained this extended and unexplained absence with the best interests of the Parish at heart. However, after a very patient and extremely painful three months without any ongoing communication or visit from our Bishop, we humbly request of you, at this time, three things:

1. We urgently express our complete support for a timely and public vindication of Father Bill's good name, as this responsibility rests solely in the hands of your office.

2. We humbly ask for you to bring closure to the Parish by granting a speedy return of Father Bill to his parish family at Holy Cross. We ask this in respect of the authority that rests upon your shoulders, as Bishop of Hamburg.

3. Given the serious nature of our Parish situation we are requesting a meeting with your Excellency, attended by five parish representatives including the parish council president, to have an opportunity to discuss with you Father Bill's innocence and the steps that can be taken toward the restoration of his good name and his return to Holy Cross Parish.

We firmly believe and acknowledge that our priest has been proven to be innocent of the alleged charges against him. We understand that the false accusations of Father Bill's computer containing criminal gay pornography web sites in the web history to be unwarranted. We understand that after a thorough investigation that included an extensive search of Father Bill's computer hard drive, the Livingston County Prosecutor and Michigan State Police have not filed criminal charges against Father Bill.

Perfectly credible reasons exist why various questionable web sites were found on Father Bill's hard drive. We are convinced that not only is Father Bill not guilty of anything criminal, but that he is not morally culpable for any wrongdoing either. In light of this, it is imperative that Father Bill be vindicated by the Diocese of Hamburg. It is a question of justice. We want to ensure that proper steps are being taken to restore the good and holy name of our priest, Father Wesley Thomas. We believe that if some of our parishioners met with you, this process on behalf of Father Bill Thomas could be sped up. Parish life at Holy Cross is sorely strained and diminished in the absence of Father Bill's leadership, pastoral care, spiritual direction and loyal friendship.

In addition, **we are aware that these allegations were brought forth by a Parish staff member, who entered the Pastor's private quarters without permission for an unwarranted time of 18 months. This staff person has a leadership position in the parish and without Father Bill's innocence resolved this creates an atmosphere of tension.** Innocent parishioners are being manipulated by hearsay and a one-sided presentation of this situation. I'm sure you can imagine, Your Excellency, the extreme strain on parish life and we are concerned that the whole controversy may become public knowledge if Father Bill is not quickly restored.

The strain at the parish has come to a boiling point, as such we are reaching out to you as our guiding light and shepherd and hope that you will sincerely offer some compassion to your hurting sheep and allow us a chance to meet with you in Hamburg. We are hurting and desperately seek your assistance.

In expressing our pain, we in no way minimize the fine efforts of Father Steven Klanyi, Canonical Administrator, who has been filling in during Father Bill's absence. While Father Steve has done an admirable job in a difficult situation, there is simply no substitute for a parish's pastor- just as there is no real substitute for a family's father.

In closing, we would like to share some examples of Father Bill's great pastoral care at Holy Cross, just a few highlights of the many accomplishments and qualities that make this situation even more heartbreaking:

• Father Bill's sincere obedience to the teachings of the Catholic Church and the Church's Hierarchy' even when defending this Truth requires much courage in the face of great adversity. Our role-model pastor stood at the forefront of efforts to maintain the sanctity of Marriage during last year's "One Man, One Woman" initiative, and his courageous example gave us hope that we lay people could also stand up for Catholic values and have a real impact on our society. With the miraculous success of this effort, Father Bill showed us that the Truth will prevail and set us free, if only we have the courage to defend it. This is only one example of Father Bill's willingness to teach us, in word and in deed, the unvarnished Truth in all areas of our lives as Catholics - even when this Truth is uncomfortable for us.

• Father Bill's devoted love of the Mass and the Eucharist and great respect for all the Sacraments. Father Bill's respect and devotion to the Mass is well-known, and we are deeply grateful for his founding of Perpetual Adoration at Holy Cross, which has brought many great blessings to our parish family. Father Bill offers Confession three times a week as a visible affirmation of the need for God's grace offered through sacramental absolution, and he is an unparalleled supporter of all aspects of sacramental life.

• Father Bill is an ardent supporter of solid, lifelong Catholic Education - Father Bill founded our Holy Cross Roman Catholic School in accordance with the Holy Cross Mission statement to educate our parish family, while also maintaining strong support and assistance for home schoolers and public school children in our parish family. His commitment to Catholic education does not stop with our youth, but extends throughout an unsurpassed array of adult education initiatives as well.

• Father Bill has made Holy Cross a missionary parish - With Father Bill's support and leadership, Holy Cross is active in outreach ministry to Mexico and Dominican Republic, helping those in dire need both materially and spiritually. Father Bill's local outreach includes his support of WJ Maxey Boys Training School, his chaplaincy of Courage, a very active St. Vincent DePaul group, Catholic Social Services, and numerous other examples of Father Bill leading our parish to carry out the vision of the Communion of Saints.

We are aware that you have submitted your mandatory request to retire as Bishop of Hamburg, and our hearts are heavy with such uncertainty hanging over two great spiritual fathers - Bishop and our Pastor. However, if indeed it is God's will that you soon leave us, what an opportunity this situation presents! - to make one of your final acts of courage and pastoral care as our Bishop the restoration of our parish family, uniting Holy Cross Parish again with its pastor, Father Wesley Thomas.

We sincerely hope that a meeting with you will be scheduled as soon as possible. Please contact Mr. Mike Drenski, president of the Parish Council' whose contact information is below.

Respectfully and prayerfully yours,

The undersigned parishioners of Holy Cross Roman Catholic Church as follows:

The letter was signed by those present at the meeting. For reasons known only to him, Devlock did not sign the document. It is important to note, that the Diocese did not inform me of the letter or its intention to malign me. I obtained a copy of the document through a concerned parishioner. I issued the following letter to the Diocese in response:

August 18, 2006

Deacon Mark Kurry
Diocese of Hamburg

Dear Mike,

In my ongoing effort to keep you informed regarding our parish I submit this letter.

The agenda to target me for removal for having to report Father Thomas's behavior is as impassioned as ever among those who regularly associate with him and support his denial. I knew that a letter existed signed by several parishioners that demanded the return of Father Thomas. Until the Attorney Grievance Commission shared this letter with me as part of Jude Devlock's defense, I did not know of the paragraph that implicates me as the aggressor and accuser. A copy of this letter is enclosed, although I know obviously the Diocese has it already in their possession.

What is unfolding here is clear and shameful harassment of a whistleblower. My employment situation at the parish is under repeated attack from these people, some of whom, such as Teresa Panky are using their position of influence on the Parish Council to sustain and qualify their campaign of harassment. We saw this same scenario unfolding before with Jude Devlock's involvement prior to his departure. Mrs. Panky has a close relationship with Mr. Devlock. They were inseparable in the early days of this crisis. Mrs. Panky's efforts to discredit the staff and our service have resulted in the resignation of our bookkeeper just this morning. Stella volunteered 40 hours a week out of love for this parish. She is in her eighties and can no longer endure the sustained hateful effort on behalf of a few to discredit her.

The Parish Council met last night. Teresa Panky seized the opportunity once again to cast a shroud of suspicion and doubt on the staff of this parish. The primary target, of course is me, followed by Stella Campbell and the Finance Council. The parish finances have become the vehicle for this abusive campaign. For the second time consecutively, the meeting was never brought under control. Also for the second time the size of our "administrative" staff was alluded to as a reason for our financial situation. Mrs. Panky is utilizing her status as a CPA in conjunction with my admittedly limited financial training to appear qualified to defame our efforts to manage the business practices of this church. I firmly believe that Teresa and Michael Panky, Linda and Pat Orli, John and Denise Noland, Paul and Michelle Radley, Bill Doory, Mike Drenski and a few others would be satisfied witnessing the complete destruction of this faith community if that becomes necessary for the realization of their goal. This is further evidenced, I believe, in the fact that most of them have ceased all personal financial support of their parish.

I have suggested to Father Steve, who has witnessed this that perhaps under the extreme circumstances, our Parish Council needs to be suspended until such a time as this malice subsides.

This shameful agenda that is traumatizing our parish is being engineered with purpose and it must stop.

Thank you very much. God bless you.

Patrick J. Flynn
Business Manager

cc: Fr. Steve Klanyi

The diocese had a solemn obligation to protect my rights under Canon Law[3]. Rather, they did what they do best - nothing. They chose their favorite tool - silence.

The State Police report, once released, revealed that the assumptions made in the letter to the Bishop were false, considerably careless, and irresponsible. Nevertheless, not one of the signers has expressed any apology or regret to me regarding their endorsement of the letter. Among the signers, the vast majority either had no sons, or their sons were not of the age that would classify them as potential victims. In other words, Father Thomas' dangerous interests and desires would not affect their families. How incredibly selfish! Also noted was the interesting and somewhat chilling fact that among the signers, seven of them either had a personal experience of sexual abuse or had family members who were either molested or convicted of sexual molestation. I suspect these people defended Father's predatory behavior because to do otherwise would have meant facing their own demons. I imagined them struggling with the concept that if

Father was guilty of this sin, than what about my uncle who proclaims his innocence? What about my accused brother? What about my dad?

Due to mounting concerns in the face of this disgusting agenda, I contacted Father Dormond at his office at Courage/Encourage and asked him if he would author a letter in testimony of my character and my willingness and determination to do the right thing. Father told me he would write the letter immediately and send it as soon as he could. I received the letter of support from Father Dormond on January 27. The text of the letter follows:

The Paulist Fathers
415 West 59th Street
New York, NY 10019

Jan. 25, 2006

To whom this may concern:

During the year of 2004-2005 in which I was Acting Director of Courage (Fr. Harrison being on Sabbatical), Mr. Patrick Flynn called me with a problem affecting the Courage Movement. His Pastor is the regional Director of the Courage movement in the area.

Mr. Flynn is Business Manager of Holy Cross parish in Michigan and as such does many services for the parish. During his work he came across some pornographic materials on the Pastor's personal computer. Being concerned about this finding, Mr. Flynn brought it to the attention of the Pastor who denied any knowledge of the matter and suggested that someone else might have been involved but not he.

However, material (of an increasingly serious level) continued to accumulate on the PC of the Pastor, including some kind of application for "membership" in a homosexual network. Mr. Flynn reported a noticeable lethargy in the spiritual life of the parish. Additionally, there was a teenage boy who did his homework in the parish under the tutelage of the pastor. Suddenly, the mother of the boy pulled the boy out of the parish and will not allow him to study at the rectory any longer. This did not escape the notice of Mr. Flynn who has children himself.

69

Mr. Flynn whose livelihood depends on the Pastor, his employer, became seriously conflicted about the matter. He had affection for the Pastor but had deep feelings of responsibility to the Church and the parish. Fearfully, he devised his own plan of revealing the situation in the internal forum where he would be protected from any kind of retaliation. He made Confession to a priest of the Diocese who took the matter ultimately to the Bishop who initially told the Pastor to get rid of that material on the PC and in effect, "Straighten up and fly right."

Ultimately, the Bishop assured Mr. Flynn that his job is safe. Apparently, the addiction continued and the Bishop learning of this development, removed the Pastor from his post and sent the Pastor back home in another area, three hours drive from the Parish. The matter had to be sent to civil authorities who now possess (what was believed to be) the original hard drive for analysis. No criminal charges are imminent. Any problem is to be dealt with by the Church. Meanwhile, the Pastor somehow had removed the offending drive and replaced it with a totally new one.

Currently, the Pastor reversing himself on his original denial, now claims that he did this viewing of many hours merely in obedience to Fr. Harrison who asked him to do this on behalf of Courage and for research. Fr. Harrison told me yesterday (1/24/06) that this is not true and suggests that the Pastor be sent for "rehabilitation" for at least one year. In fact, Fr. Harrison is now concerned to replace the Pastor as the on-site rep for Courage.

From what I can hear from Mr. Flynn, I believe his presentation. I do not see any evidence of lying either now or in previous phone conversations. I am further impressed with his need be honest and his need to take the great risk of doing the right thing (as he sees it). It took great courage to face the shunning from people who believe that he framed the Pastor. He reached a point where it was more important to speak up for his conviction than to have the approval of people. Justice and fairness are terribly important as are the spiritual needs of the Church.

The above is what I know of this painful and sad situation.

(Rev.) James B. Dormond csp. Ph. D.

I was truly grateful for Father Dormond's confidence in me and his counsel during this painful time.

Shortly after receiving Father Dormond's letter, a woman from the parish came into my office to speak with me regarding the whole situation. Immediately I detected contempt in her attitude. Although she expressed that she was only interested in the truth and claimed to be objective, it was obvious she was not going to entertain any notion that Father Thomas was capable of any wrongdoing. I gave her a copy of Father Dormond's letter. She was unmoved. She then left me with a copy of a book written by St. John Vianney about the sacredness of the priesthood. Apparently, in her narrow judgement, she was convinced that the book would help me to see the err of my ways and repent from smearing the good name of a priest. She immediately took the letter and gave it to Jude Devlock. Apparently it was now necessary for Devlock to close this valve of support for me if he was ever going to continue to spin the truth. It is apparent that Devlock's position as an attorney would afford him an interesting level of intimidation. Devlock's behavior from this point would indicate that he is completely unconcerned with the mortal sin involved with intentionally trying to destroy the reputation and character of an innocent man in an effort to protect a predator.

Father Dormond called and left a voicemail message on my cell phone on February 18. He was alarmed. He said that he received a package in the mail from the law firm of Devlock & Devlock. In the correspondence, Father said, were direct and condemning insults against him by Jude Devlock. Father said that Jude called him "*arrogant, ignorant and lacking in masculinity.*" He also stated that Devlock also referred to me in many derogatory ways. Father then said that the package finally contained a threat from Devlock to sue him for libel for writing the letter on my behalf. The long voicemail concluded with a plea for me to call him as soon as I could.

I connected with Father Dormond by phone on February 20. Father reiterated the details of the package in our conversation. I tried to calm Father down. I reminded him of his own words to me that when this whole affair was finally reported that all hell would break loose. I told him all about Devlock and his dark role in covering Father Thomas' sin. It apparently surprised Father

Dormond that people could choose to do such evil. He had been a priest for nearly 50 years. It should not have surprised him at all. I encouraged him to remain undaunted by the shameful attacks of this depraved bully.

On March 4, a fax arrives at the church office for me from Devlock. The short message:

> Dear Pat:
>
> Fr. James Dormond sent me an email message to you, through me because as he explains in his message, he doesn't have your email address. I have attached a copy of his email.
>
> Jude Devlock

The attached message:

> Mr. Devlock,
>
> Since I do not have Patrick Flynn's email address, I ask you to forward this to him.
>
> Mr. Flynn,
>
> I urgently ask you to discontinue the circulation of a letter I wrote to you at your request. This letter was written in good faith and not intended for circulation but only for your private file that you could prove you did contact Courage last spring and that I only reflected back what you told me. The situation was vague since there was no one in particular you had in mind. You agreed this was the understanding in a telephone call on 2/20/06. I called you in disappointment at said circulation. You also denied in that call that you had circulated it. This circulation has resulted in a direct harm to me and my name. Fr. John Harrison has advised me that he is completely in back of me and that I am to inform you that legal action may be taken if you do not immediately cease circulation of this letter intended only to protect you in the event of any future attack on you. I agreed to this in good faith and that was all.
>
> Rev JB Dormond

Interesting indeed that such a conflicting and ambiguous message should come to me from Fr. Dormond through the same lawyer that bullied and threatened him just days before. For the record, Father was in possession of all my contact information including both my email addresses. This is further testimony of the rot permeating through the leaders of the Catholic Church who are at worst complicit in the violation of the innocents or at best just too frightened to stand against its supporting evil.

This betrayal cut through me as deeply and as hurtfully as any saber could. I really trusted and looked up to Fr. Dormond for all this time and had certainly not pegged him as one who would fold at the first sign of spiritual battle. Following this all my emails and voicemails to Father went unanswered. It is not uncommon, however for a popular priest, author and acting head of a nationwide Catholic ministry to be so consumed and focused on his celebrity to consider actually converting all the strong words into courageous and direct action.

By the above, it seems Mr. Devlock is quite skilled in the shameful tactics of intimidation of the weak. The combination of tepid leaders and depraved manipulators is a very effective cocktail for the production of pure victimization.

Chapter Eight
The State Police Report Reveals Much

The Report from the Michigan State Police investigation regarding Father Thomas' computer internet misconduct is available to the public via the Freedom of Information Act. The entire text of the report follows. The voids in the report depict personal information removed by the Michigan State Police prior to public release. Names have been changed for consistency.

Michigan Department of State Police	ORIGINAL DATE Tue, Sep 13, 2005		INCIDENT NO. 012-0005383-05 (DB)	
ORIGINAL INCIDENT REPORT	TIME RECEIVED 1613		FILE CLASS 36004	
	WORK UNIT MSP BRIGHTON		COUNTY Livingston	
COMPLAINANT Mark Kurry			TELEPHONE NO. (517)242-	
ADDRESS: STREET AND NO.		CITY	STATE	ZIP CODE
INCIDENT STATUS Open				

Sex Offense

INFORMATION:

I was contacted by Prosecutor David Morse reference a complaint involving a Catholic priest at a parish in Livingston County. Prosecutor Morse stated that the Diocese of Hamburg had contacted him after they became aware that the priest was visiting web sites that may involve child pornography. Prosecutor Morse stated that there was a possibility that the priest may have had an inappropriate relationship with a juvenile from the parish.

Prosecutor Morse gave me a packet of information that was given to him by the Diocese.

VENUE:

LIVINGSTON COUNTY , BRIGHTON TWP
AT OR NEAR: MSP BRIGHTON

DATE & TIME:

TUE, SEP 13, 2005

COMPLAINANT:

NAM: Mark Kurry
P.O. Box/Building: DIOCESE OF Hamburg
NBR: DIR: RAC: ETH:
STR: SEX: OPS:
SFX: DOB: SSN:
CTY: ST: HGT: SID:
TXH: ZIP: WGT: FBI:
TXW: (517)242-   HAI: MNU:
MB: EYE: PRN:

PAGE 1 of 3	INVESTIGATED BY D/SGT SEAN FURLONG	REPORTED BY	REVIEWED BY

INTERVIEW COMPLAINANT:

Kurry is an attorney with the Diocese of Lansing. Mr. Kurry is my point of contact with the Diocese. Kurry is the representative that gave the material related to this complaint to David Morse.

POSSIBLE CRIMINAL ACTS:

The Diocese was notified by a parishioner that Father Wesley Thomas of Holy CROSS Church in Green Oak Township was looking at inappropriate web sites. The parishioner, Patrick Flynn, discovered this while working on the priests computer. Flynn provided the Archdiocese with a listing of the web sites. The web site names give the impression that Father Thomas is attempting to view child pornography.

The Diocese also gave Prosecutor Morse a letter of complaint from a parishioner reference Father Thomas' involvement in their son's life. The letter indicated that Father Thomas allowed the juvenile full access to the rectory, gave gifts to the juvenile, and allowed the juvenile to drink alcohol at the rectory. The letter also indicates that Father Thomas may have allowed the child to sleep at the rectory and Father Thomas may have lied to the parents about the child being at the rectory.

SUSPECT:

```
NAM:           WESLEY THOMAS
P.O. Box/Building: HOLY  CROSSCHURCH        RAC: W        ETH:
NBR:        DIR:
STR:
SFX:
CTY: BRIGHTON          ST: MI
TXH:                   ZIP:
TXW:
```

INTERVIEW SUSPECT:

The suspect has not yet been interviewed.

ACTION TAKEN:

I contacted the Computer Crimes Unit in SECID Livonia. D/Spl. Thomas Kish was given the list of web sites that were visited by Father Thomas. Kish checked the web sites and informed me that the majority of the web sites were no longer active. Kish advised that the web sites that he was able to investigate were adult gay porn sites.

Further investigation will be done to enable me to seize the rectory computer. I will also contact the family in the letter of complaint sent to the Archdiocese to determine if any inappropriate contact was made between the suspect and the child.

| PAGE | INVESTIGATED BY D/SGT SEAN FURLONG | REPORTED BY | REVIEWED BY |
| 2 of 3 | | | |

ORIGINAL DATE	INCIDENT NO.
Tue, Sep 13, 2005	012-0005383-05 (DB)
TIME RECEIVED	FILE CLASS
1613	36004

STATUS:

Open - Pending Further Investigation.

Michigan Department of State Police	ORIGINAL DATE Tue, Sep 13, 2005	INCIDENT NO. 012-0005383-05 (DB)
SUPPLEMENTAL INCIDENT REPORT 0001	SUPPLEMENTARY DATE Wed, Oct 12, 2005	FILE CLASS 36004

INCIDENT STATUS
Open

Sex Offense Other

JOURNAL:

10-7-05   Furlong   I.R. Pends further investigation.

INFORMATION:

Since the original report was completed, Father Thomas was relieved of his duties at Holy Cross . Due to the nature of this complaint, the Diocese of Hamburg decided to place an interim priest at Holy Cross . Father Thomas was notified of this change and he left Holy Cross two days after he was notified.

During this time, an investigator from the Attorney General Internet Crimes Against Children Unit contacted the parish and inquired about this complaint. This investigator, S/A Peplinski, did not inquire if an investigation was already ongoing and made contact with employees at the parish. By the time S/A Peplinksi became aware that I was doing an investigation, his actions at the parish caused Father Thomas to become aware that a criminal investigation was initiated.

Due to these issues, Father Thomas had a number of days to destroy potential evidence before he was removed from Holy Cross .

SUSPECT:

NAM: WESLEY THOMAS
P.O. Box/Building: HOLY CROSSCHURCH   RAC: W   ETH:
NBR: DIR:
STR:
SFX:
CTY: BRIGHTON   ST: MI
TXH: ZIP:

SEIZE COMPUTER:

I received consent to take the computer from the rectory used by Father Thomas. On October 18, 2005, I obtained a signed consent to search the computer from the new interim priest, Father Klanyi . This signed consent will be attached as an external document.

PAGE 1 of 7	INVESTIGATED BY D/SGT SEAN M FURLONG	REPORTED BY	REVIEWED BY

COMPUTER CRIMES UNIT:

I took the seized computer to SECID Computer Crime unit. I was contacted on October 25, 2005, by the computer crimes unit. They informed me that the computer had been cleared of any and all data. They informed me that the computer was devoid of any data. They informed me that the hard drive had either been cleaned by a professional with professional software or the hard drive was removed and replaced with a new hard drive.

CONTACT - INTERVIEW POSSIBLE VICTIM:

The Diocese of Hamburg had given me a copy of a letter that was sent to them by the parents of Alex Sanchez. The Sanchez' are members of Holy Cross and they have two children. Mrs. Sanchez wrote a letter to the Diocese complaining about problems that they were having with Father Thomas and the involvement that Father Thomas had in Alex's life.

The letter from the Sanchez complained that Father Thomas was interfering in Alex's life, contrary to what the parents wanted or tried to do. The letter contained many complaints and allegations, including that Father Thomas supplied Alex with gifts, lied to the parents, and hid Alex when his parents were looking for him.

Due to the nature of the web sites that Father Thomas was believed to be viewing and the involvement Father Thomas had in Alex's life, I decided to interview Alex Sanchez. The interview with Alex was as a possible witness to child pornography on the rectory computer and any physical contact Father Thomas may have had with

POSSIBLE WITNESS AND/OR VICTIM:

NAM

RAC: ETH:

INTERVIEW WITNESS:

I interviewed Alex in the interview room at the Brighton State Police Post. I told Alex that I was interviewing him as a potential witness and victim. I informed Alex that he was free to leave at any time if he became uncomfortable or he did not want to talk to me.

I informed Alex that I was investigating possible criminal activity at Holy Cross Church. I told Alex that I was aware that and I was interested in what he saw and what he did

PAGE	INVESTIGATED BY D/SGT SEAN M FURLONG	REPORTED BY	REVIEWED BY
2 of 7			

I asked   : for Father Thomas and how long his family had been members at Holy Cross.   informed me that his family had moved to his current residence when   He stated that his house is   and his family joined the parish shortly after moving to the area.   informed me that his family was active in the church and he came to know Father Thomas through church activities.

stated that sometime in 2003
                    stated that Father knew

he had daily contact with Father and received his job assignments from Father.   stated that his mother felt Father was interfering in what his mother wanted in regards to   . life and issues.   stated that he has not spoken to Father since   .

stated that this was so he could look after the rectory while Father Thomas was gon   stated that he also received a work cell phone from Father and he also was assigned his own log in name and password to the rectory computer.

I asked Alex   if he would consider Father Thomas a friend. Alex   stated that he was friendly with Father and they would spend time together doing things and talking. Alex   stated that they would watch movies together in the rectory. Alex   informed me that he would mention to Father that he had seen a good movie and Father would go rent the movie and the two of them would watch it together. Alex   stated that they also went to a shooting range together Alex   informed me that Father had a couple of handguns and Father let him shoot one of the handguns.

I asked Alex   bout his use of the rectory computer. Alex   informed me that he was given his own log in name but he did not use the computer very often. Alex   stated that he mainly used the computer to download music and burn CD's. Alex   stated that he mainly used the Kazaa website to download his music.

I asked Alex   if he ever saw anything of a sexual nature on the computer or if he ever watched any pornographic videos with Father. Alex   stated that he never saw anything like that on the computer nor did he ever watch pornographic videos with Father. Alex   : stated that he never even spoke with Father about sexual related issues. Alex   informed me that he had a girlfriend and he did not talk to Father about any issues related to sex or relationships.

I asked Alex   if Father ever hugged or touched him in any manner that might be viewed as excessive or inappropriate. Alex   stated that he Father never touched him and that Father would have no reason to because   was not gay. Alex   stated that he never gave Father any indication that he was he was gay or that he wanted Father to touch him so there was no reason for Father to even try and touch him.

PAGE	INVESTIGATED BY D/SGT SEAN M FURLONG	REPORTED BY	REVIEWED BY
3 of 7			

I asked Alex why he had not spoken to Father since _____ I told Alex I thought this was odd since they had been friends and had spent so much time together. In addition, _____ and his family were still members of the parish. _____ informed me that other than his mother not wanting Father to interfere with Alex's life, he had no reason. Alex stated that he was not actively going to church and he had no reason to talk to Father.

COMPLAINANT:

NAM: **Mark Kurry**

			RAC:		ETH:
NBR:	DIR:		SEX:		OPS:
STR:			DOB:		SSN:
SFX:			HGT:		SID:
CTY:		ST:	WGT:		FBI:
TXH:		ZIP:	HAI:		MNU:
TXW: (517)342-2456			EYE:		PRN:
BU ‾‾‾					
MB:					

CONTACT COMPLAINANT:

I was contacted by the complainant on November 16, 2005. Kurry stated that a meeting with Father Thomas had been held on November 10, 2005. Kurry stated that the meeting was between a number of people and Father Thomas was represented by a Canon Law priest out of New York. Kurry informed me that Father Thomas showed up at the meeting with fellow parishioner, Jude Devlock . Devlock is a Holy Cross parish council member and he is also an attorney.

Kurry stated that Father Thomas and Devlock were questioned as to why Devlock was at the meeting. Kurry informed me that both Father Thomas and Devlock stated that Devlock was only present as a friend and to provide support to Father Thomas. Kurry stated that during this meeting, Devlock made a reference to the hard drive from the computer that I had seized and examined. Devlock stated during the meeting that he had removed the hard drive from the computer and replaced it with a new hard drive. Kurry informed me that Devlock stated that he had done this prior to my seizing the computer. Kurry stated that Jude Devlock admitted that he currently had the computer hard drive in his possession.

OBTAIN SEARCH WARRANTS:

Based on the above information provided to me by the complainant, I obtained two search warrants for the hard drive. The search warrants were for the law offices and the residence of Jude Devlock . The search warrants were signed by Judge Brennan on July 18, 2005.

PAGE 4 of 7	INVESTIGATED BY D/SGT SEAN M FURLONG	REPORTED BY	REVIEWED BY

WITNESS / SUSPECT:

NAM: ROBERT STEVEN PAVLOCK

RAC: W   ETH:

CONTACT INTERVIEW DEVLOCK :

After obtaining the search warrants Tpr. Sura and I made contact with Jude Devlock at his office on Grand River. Devlock informed me that he had been hoping to talk to the investigators and he was glad to assist us in any way possible. Devlock informed me that he wanted to talk to me because he had a computer hard drive that was taken from Father Thomas' computer. I asked Devlock were the hard drive was located and he informed me that the hard drive was at his residence in Hartland. I requested that Devlock accompany me to his residence so that I could take the hard drive. I drove Devlock to his residence where he retrieved the hard drive and gave it to me. Devlock did this willing and the search warrants were never served or disclosed to

I interviewed Devlock reference his involvement with Father Thomas and his possession of the hard drive. Devlock informed me that he is a member of Holy Cross Church and he is also a member of the Parish Council. Devlock stated that he has known Father for a number of years but he did not characterize Father Thomas as a close friend. Devlock stated that he first became aware of an investigation when Father Thomas called him while Father was driving back from a meeting with the Bishop in Hamburg. Devlock stated that Father called and asked if Devlock knew how to completely erase a computer hard drive. Devlock stated that Father told him that some allegations were made against him reference pornography on the computer and the Bishop wanted Father to clean out the computer and get rid of any pornography.

Devlock stated that he told Father that he would try to find out how the erase a computer hard drive for him. Devlock informed me that he discovered that there was no way to completely erase a hard drive and the best course of action was to replace the hard drive. Devlock informed me that he ordered a new hard drive from Gateway computers and had it shipped to his law offices. Devlock provided me with a copy of the bill and the shipping receipt. The hard drive was ordered on September 21, 2005. Devlock stated that the hard drive was shipped to his office a few days after it was ordered. Devlock informed me that after the new hard drive arrived, he went to the rectory at Holy Cross and he assisted Father Thomas in taking the old hard drive out and putting the new hard drive in.

Devlock stated that Father Thomas took possession of the old hard drive after it was removed. Devlock stated that he was told by Father Thomas that Father took the hard drive and he gave it to Dr. Gold at Mother of God College in Ann Arbor.
Devlock stated that Dr. Gold had the hard drive for a short period of time before he shipped it back to Father Thomas. Devlock stated that he was unsure why Dr. Gold shipped the hard drive back to Father Thomas.

PAGE	INVESTIGATED BY	REPORTED BY	REVIEWED BY
5 of 7	D/SGT SEAN M FURLONG		

82

Devlock stated that after receiving the hard drive back, Father Thomas left the hard drive at Jude Devlock's residence when Father was there for a visit. Devlock stated that he kept the hard drive in its original unopened shipping package and he placed it in his home office. The package was still unopened when I seized the hard drive from Pavlock.

Devlock stated that since Father had been removed from Holy Cross., Father had stayed at Devlock's residence on a number of occasions. Devlock informed me that Father has a residence in Bear Lake but when he has come back to the area he has stayed at Devlock's residence. Devlock stated that he is aware why Father was removed from Holy Cross but he does not believe the allegations. Devlock stated that Father was put in charge of a ministry that provides guidance to catholics who are gay. Devlock stated that he was certain that anything of that nature on the computer was related to research and work that Father Thomas was doing for that ministry. Devlock stated that he was certain that Father Thomas was not a pedophile. Devlock informed me that he believed that the allegations made against Father Thomas were part of some infighting between certain members of the parish.

ACTION TAKEN:

The seized hard drive was turned over to D/Tpr. MacArthur of the Computer Crime Unit in Livonia. D/Tpr. MacArthur examined the hard drive and contacted me when she was finished. She informed me that she found evidence of searches for child pornography but she did not discover any images that would support a Child Abusive Material charge. MacArthur stated that rest of the hard drive contained a fair amount of adult gay pornography, which is not illegal to possess.

D/Tpr. MacArthur will be sending me a report along with returning the hard drive to me. This complaint will remain open - pending Computer Crime Unit reports and property.

PROPERTY:

SEIZED BY: SEAN FURLONG
Prop 0003 - Type: Computer Hardware/Software Qty: 1 Article Type: Hard Disk Value: $70.00
Descrp: 40 GB ATA / 100 WESTERN DIGITAL CAVIAR HARD DRIVE
Obtained From:
    JUDE DEVLOCK'S RESIDENCE

SEIZED BY: SEAN FURLONG
Prop 0001 - Type: Computer Hardware/Software Qty: 1 Article Type: Computer Brand: Gateway 2000
Model: 300X S/N: 0029942615 Value: $100.00
Obtained From:
HOLY CROSS CHURCH

Prop 0002 - Type: Computer Hardware/Software Qty: 1 Article Type: Computer Brand: Gateway 2000
Model: 5300 S/N: 6366BR403596 Value: $100.00 Recovered Value: $100.00

PAGE 6 of 7	INVESTIGATED BY D/SGT SEAN M FURLONG	REPORTED BY	REVIEWED BY

ORIGINAL DATE	INCIDENT NO.
Tue, Sep 13, 2005	012-0005383-05 (DB)
SUPPLEMENTARY DATE	FILE CLASS
Wed, Oct 12, 2005	36004

Obtained From:
HOLY CROSS CHURCH

STATUS:

Open - Pending Computer Crime Unit report and property.

PAGE	INVESTIGATED BY	REPORTED BY	REVIEWED BY
7 of 7	D/SGT SEAN M FURLONG		

Michigan Department of State Police	ORIGINAL DATE Tue, Sep 13, 2005	INCIDENT NO. 012-0005383-05 (DB)
SUPPLEMENTAL INCIDENT REPORT 0002	SUPPLEMENTARY DATE Mon, Jan 23, 2006	FILE CLASS 36004

INCIDENT STATUS
Open

Sex Offense Other

JOURNAL:

12-12-05   Furlong   Rev Supp #1. Pends Computer Crime Unit report and property.

COMPLAINANT:

NAM: Mark Kurry

NBR:	DIR:		RAC:		ETH:	
STR:			SEX:		OPS:	
SFX:			DOB:		SSN:	
CTY:		ST:	HGT:		SID:	
TXH:		ZIP:	WGT:		FBI:	
TXW: (517)342-			HAI:		MNU:	
BU:			EYE:		PRN:	
MB:						

SUSPECT:

NAM: WESLEY THOMAS
P.O. Box/Building: HOLY CROSS CHURCH   RAC: W   ETH:
NBR: DIR:
STR:
SFX:
CTY: BRIGHTON   ST: MI
TXH: ZIP:
TXW:

CCU REPORT:

The report from the Computer Crime Unit (CCU-156-05) was received and is attached as an external
document to this report. The computer crime unit did not find any images on the computer hard drive in an
area that is considered prosecutable. They did find possible child pornography in the computers unallocated
hard drive space. Images in this area of the computer are not considered prosecutable due to the fact that the
computer crime unit cannot positively state how the images were placed in this area and it does not meet the
legal definition of possession of child pornography.

PAGE	INVESTIGATED BY D/SGT SEAN M FURLONG	REPORTED BY	REVIEWED BY
1 of 2			

ACTION TAKEN:

This complaint will be closed. There were no images located on the computer that can be used for a criminal charge and there is no known victim of any type of assault.

PROPERTY RETURN:

All property that was seized in this incident were returned to Father Klanyi   on Thursday, January 26, 2005.

STATUS:

Closed

MSP SECID Computer Crimes Unit	ORIGINAL DATE Tue, Nov 22, 2005	INCIDENT NO. CCU-0000156-05 (FU)
SUPPLEMENTAL INCIDENT REPORT 0001	SUPPLEMENTARY DATE Tue, Nov 22, 2005	FILE CLASS 37000

INCIDENT STATUS
Open

POSSESSION OF CHILD PORNOGRAPHY

JOURNAL:

11/22/05	D/Sgt. Kish	I/R pends forensic
11/23/05	D/Sgt. Kish	AICS #1 removed for imaging by D/Spl. MacArthur
11/30/05	D/Spl MacArthur	Forensic exam completed. Item #1 removed from property for pickup by Detective Sgt Furlong.

FORENSIC EXAM SUMMARY:

Acquired Media

On 11/23/05, the Western Digital 40GB HDD, serial number WMAATA350701 was connected to a "Fast Bloc" write blocking device to preserve and acquire the data contained on it. Encase software was used to acquire the media, which created proprietary forensic image files onto the Forensic drive, preserving the seized media in it's original state. These forensic image files contain a bit-stream image of the original media, which was verified as an exact duplicate of the original hard drive. The exam was conducted on the exact duplicate image, using Encase version 5.03 and Forensic Toolkit version 1.60.

Operating System Information

The system's registry files reported the operating system, Windows XP, was registered to " Wesley Thomas." The system had one unique user named "Owner" - full user name " Wesley Thomas." The time zone settings were set for Eastern Standard Time.

Images and Videos

The hard drive contained a total of approximately 16,500 graphics, a dozen video files and 8,000 images in unallocated space which were all reviewed for instances of child pornography.

A total of 7 images were bookmarked as suspected child pornography which were all located in unallocated space. This means these images were deleted from the directory and from the Recycle Bin. Due to the fact that these images were no longer tracked by a directory, there are no time and date stamps associated with these files nor is their origin known.

Embedded Image Files in Emails

Approximately 300 image files embedded in emails were reviewed for any references to child pornography with none being located.

Emails

Several emails were bookmarked as they referenced 'teen' and or 'young' pornography. One of the emails from ' Wesley Thomas' makes reference to a membership to the on-line web site 'Boyscherries.com.'

Saved Passwords for Pornography Web Sites

The operating system's registry documented saved passwords for three web sites, 'Boycherries.com,' 'Twinks.com' and '1on1.militaryguy.com.' These web sites were accessed by this examiner to ascertain if the

PAGE	INVESTIGATED BY D/SGT THOMAS P KISH #335	REPORTED BY	REVIEWED BY
1 of 2			

87

sites contained child pornography. Each site made claims that their pornography uses 18+ year old models and requires users to sign in as members prior to viewing.

Due to the fact that membership is required to view their pornography, this examiner was unable to ascertain if the site includes child pornography.

Web Cache – Internet History

Several Internet web address were bookmarked for their content relating to 'teen,' 'boy' or 'young' pornography. Some of the web addresses appear to be Internet searches for child pornography. The system's registry also documented the user account of " Wesley Thomas" Yahoo and Google search history, which contained reference to 'teen' pornography.

STATUS:

Open, pends release of property

PAGE 2 of 2	INVESTIGATED BY D/SGT THOMAS P KISH #335	REPORTED BY	REVIEWED BY

88

I, besides Administrative Assistant am also the unofficial IT technician of the parish.

July, 2004: While tending to a technical support issue on Fr. Thomas' computer at the rectory, I noticed a recent MSN search had been done on gay male sex. During the same time I noticed many spam emails of very explicit sexual nature that appeared to be opened and read. At that time period, Father had employed a parish teen to do odd jobs at the rectory. Father had recently before that dismissed another teen that he employed who had day and night access to the rectory.

I was troubled by this to a high degree and hoped that perhaps it was one of the teens who had conducted this search. I hope that you can understand that I was not going to bring this before the diocese of Hamburg unless I was absolutely sure there was a serious problem and not just a large misunderstanding. I decided I would speak to a priest in Melbourne Beach, Florida while I was on vacation seeking anonymously protected advice on this matter. The priest told me that I must inform Father Bill that I discovered this. I did so when I returned to Michigan. Father seemed shocked when I showed him the search on his computer. He asked me who had access to the computer that would do this. I told him that no one on the parish staff had access. I then asked him if the teen who he had currently employed was ever allowed to use the computer. He said no. I do know that the previous teen that worked at the rectory did have access to Father's computer. Father had me set up a screen name for him. But, the suspicious search that I discovered was conducted long after that teen had left Father's employ.

I decided I would just monitor the computer's history from time to time and just see what happens.

August, 2004: During a routine search, I uncovered that 8 of the 25 previous web searches were of a sexually suspicious nature.

March, 2005: The history of Father's computer reveals numerous websites visited. I tried to print the screen showing the searches but realized that is not possible. I wrote down what was on the history list. All of the following were dot coms.
Adultfriendfinder
Allfreegay
Bad-movies
Boymegaplex
Boys3D
Boysextoons
Boysfirsttime
Boysgonebad
Boys-pissing
Boystation
Circlejerkboys
Cutelatinboys

89

Formen.darktech
Free-gay-boys
Gaymaturexxx
Gaybigcockxxx
Gayblinddatesex
Gayfamilyincest
Gayhentiasex
Gaymilitarysex
Gaympegclub
Gayorgyxxx
Gayvideoxxx
Giantgaycocks
Hisclub
Hisfirsthugecock
Hunglikeme
Incestbrothers
Lilboysroom
Malepayperview
Musclemenxxx
Mygaylinks
Ohboys
Pixporn
Sexarchive
Streetbaitgalleries
Teenagetwinks
Twinksforcash
Twinkspix
Xtcmale
Xxxdateseeq

March, 2005: I was so deeply burdened with this discovery that I felt it was necessary to confide in someone. I chose our Pastoral Coordinator, Michael Wilson . I chose Michael because I know him to be an honorable man who loves Father as I do and would never do anything to hurt him. Michael is also a licensed counselor.

I decided that I should begin to photograph any evidence of this activity using the church's digital camera. The camera does seem to have trouble focusing on the LCD screen so many photos on the CD are duplicates of differing quality.

CD, Folder 6-7-05: Looking to the top banner, the address bar and the details in the panes of the photos show visits to boycherries.com and the fact that apparently, Father has become a member of the site.

CD, Folder 6-13-05: This shows a photo of Father's Dish Network bill detailing a Playboy pay-per-view order.

CD Folder 7-8-05: We see here several hours spent on line as a member of boycherries.com on July 4th and June 30th.

CD Folder 7-25-05: We see here several hours spent on line as a member of boycherries.com on July 14th, 15th, and 19th.

The loose photos that are not in folders on the CD reveal visits to adultactioncam.com, a most troubling visit to facialabberent.com where a page was opened that was titled: Meet a hottie and hook up. This might indicate that Father is connecting with other people on the internet. It was at this juncture that I knew I had to approach the diocese.

We also see in these photos more hours spent at boycherries.com as a member login on August 7th, 2nd, July 29th.

CD Folder 9-2-05: A new site is listed here called shepulledmycrank.com followed by a page to join the site. We also see a new site called vasacufeti.com with a link to another site called creamytugs.com. We also see many more hours spent on boycherries.com as a member on August 23rd, 27th. Further on we see a new site called powafowe.com and a link for a tour page and join page for hookedonteens.com viewed on the same day. Of course, this is very serious. If Father is trapped in this dreadful situation, the fact that he is the Courage and Encourage chaplain and the Catholic chaplain of the ministry at the Maxey boys prison is so very distressing and potentially dangerous.

Note: I researched the site called boycherries.com. I went no further than its index page. On that page the sites content and purpose is explained. It is a video and photo site depicting boys being violated by men for the first time. It is quite possible that this site is legal whereas the "boys" are actually over 18 but just appear younger. If the site is illegal and the photos are of minors, then merely visiting the site and subscribing to its contents as a member would be a serious crime.

I must say for myself that coming to you is without a doubt the most difficult thing I have ever had to do in my life. I love Father and he has been good to me and my family. It is apparent that he needs serious help. In our Virtus program that all parishes are asked to comply with, we are given no choice as employees of the diocese but to report such activity. But Father is our pastor and my boss, not just a co-worker. That makes this so much more heart-wrenching. Please, Monsignor, I make a heart-felt appeal to you. This job at the church is all I have to provide for my family (wife and seven children). I cannot lose my job. I need the protection of the church, please.

I have also sought anonymously the counsel of Father Dormond and Father Harrison of the Courage and Encourage Ministry in New Your City. It is also at their strong urging that I come to you now.

Father is at his cottage up north until Saturday, September 10. Michael Wilson has witnessed the contents of the computer and although he is on short-term disability, he would be available to concur with this in person if need be.

CONSENT SEARCH WARNING

I would like your permission to search your* *Two Gateway Computers*, but I hereby
advise you that: 1. You have the right to refuse.
                          2. Any evidence of criminal conduct that I find
                              will be used against you in a court of law.

WAIVER

Do you understand each of these rights I have explained to you? Understanding
these rights are you willing to allow me to search your* *Two Gateway Computers*

4:35 pm
TIME

Oct. 18, 2005
DATE

SIGNATURE

Dist. Sean Furlong
OFFICER ADVISING RIGHTS

*Insert car, house, person, etc., as applicable.

DAVID L. MORSE
LIVINGSTON COUNTY PROSECUTING ATTORNEY

Smt — Gateway Computer Model 300X Serial Number 0039943615
— Gateway Computer Model 530 Serial number 6366BR403596

92

SEARCH WARRANT

CASE NO.

POLICE AGENCY
REPORT NUMBER: 12-5383-05

D/Sgt. Sean M Furlong, Affiant(s), state(s) that:

1. *The person, place or thing to be searched is described as and is located at:*

A business office located at   Grand River in Genoa Township, Livingston County. The business is further described as being the offices of Devlock & Devlock   and it is located on the south side of Grand River, east of   Road. The business is located in the   Office Center. The office building has an orange brick exterior. The numbers   are affixed above the entrance door. A sign stating Devlock & Devlock   is to the left of the entrance door.

2. *The PROPERTY to be searched for and seized, if found, is specifically described as:*

Hard Drive from Gateway desktop computer, serial number 0029942615. The hard drive is more specifically described as a Western Digital 40-GB 5M 40GPP Hard Disk Drive [Part #5502080].

IN THE NAME OF THE PEOPLE OF THE STATE OF MICHIGAN: I have found that probable cause exists and you are commanded to make the search and seize the described property. Leave a copy of this warrant and affidavit attached and a tabulation (a written inventory) of all property taken with the person from whom the property was taken or at the premises. You are further commanded to promptly return this warrant and tabulation to the court.

Issued: _____11/18/05_____   _Theresa M Brennan_

                 Date   Judge/Magistrate

Search was made _____ and the following property was seized:
                          Date

93

AFFIDAVIT FOR
SEARCH WARRANT

CASE NO.

POLICE AGENCY
REPORT NUMBER:12-5383-05

D/Sgt. Sean Furlong, Affiant(s), state(s) that:

1. The person, place or thing to be searched is described as and is located at:

   A business office located at   E Grand River in   Township, Livingston County. The business is further described as being the offices of Devlock & Devlock and it is located on the south side of Grand River, east of   Road. The business is located in the   Office Center. The office building has an orange brick exterior. The numbers   are affixed above the entrance door. A sign stating Devlock & Devlock   is to the left of the entrance door.

2. The PROPERTY to be searched for and seized, if found, is specifically described as:

   Hard Drive from Gateway desktop computer, serial number 0029942615. The hard drive is more specifically described as a Western Digital 40-GB 5M 40GPP Hard Disk Drive [Part #5502080].

3. The FACTS establishing probable cause or the grounds for search are:

   1. The affiant is a Detective Sergeant with the Michigan State Police, assigned to the Brighton post and has been employed as a police officer for over fifteen years.

   2. Affiant states that he is investigating a complaint of possession of Child Sexually Abusive Material that has occurred at the Holy CROSSChurch in Green Oak Township, Livingston County. Affiant states that suspect in this complaint is Wesley Thomas. Wesley Thomas is the Catholic priest assigned to Holy Cross Church.

   3. Affiant states that his complainant is the Diocese of Hamburg and they are represented by their attorney, Mark Kurry .

   4. Affiant states that on September 13, 2005, Kurry provided a packet of material that was given to the Diocese by a Patrick Flynn. Patrick Flynn is employed as the Administrative Assistant at Holy Cross Church. Affiant states that this packet contained evidence that Child Sexually Abusive Material was being searched for and viewed on the computer of the church priest, Wesley Thomas

   D186̅.

   [Affiant, title & name]

Reviewed on:	Subscribed and sworn to before me on: 11/18/05
Date	Date
by: Prosecuting Official	Judge/~~Magistrate~~

94

POLICE AGENCY
REPORT NUMBER: 12-5383-05

5. Affiant states he interviewed Flynn about the material he provided to the Diocese. Flynn stated that one of his duties at the church is to provide computer support and service. Flynn stated that while working on the computer in the priest's rectory office, he observed evidence that the priest was using the internet to search for and view child pornography. Flynn stated that he observed numerous web sites in the computer history that indicated child pornography. Flynn stated that computer he observed was located in the office of the Parish rectory, which is the residence of Wesley Thomas. Flynn stated that the computer is used by Thomas and it requires that Thomas log in prior to using the computer.

6. Flynn stated that the priest used internet explorer and he visited a number of websites that clearly indicated the contents of the websites. Flynn gave me a long list of websites that were observed on the computer. The websites observed and provided by Flynn was lengthy and included the following sites:
   Boycherries.com
   Circlejerkboys.com
   Cutelatinboys.com
   Lilboysroom.com
   Boysextoons.com

7. Affiant states that the lists of web sites were sent to S/Spl. Thomas Kish of the MSP Computer Crime unit. D/Spl. Kish informed the Affiant that child pornography sites are typically only operational for a short period of time. D/Spl. Kish stated that this was done to avoid detection by law enforcement. D/Spl. Kish investigated the web sites that were known to have been visited by Wesley Thomas. D/Spl Kish advised that all the web sites that indicated child pornography were no longer operational. D/Spl. Kish indicated that through his training and experience, the website names and the short time of operation were consistent with child pornography websites.

D1 S&T. See

[Affiant, title & name]

Reviewed on:	Subscribed and sworn to before me on:
Date	11/18/05
	Date
by:	Theresa M Brennan
Prosecuting Official	Judge/Magistrate

AFFIDAVIT FOR
SEARCH WARRANT

CASE NO.

POLICE AGENCY
REPORT NUMBER:12-5383-05

8. Affiant states that due to the evidence observed by Flynn, the Diocese of Hamburg removed Thomas from Holy Cross Church pending the investigation. Affiant states Thomas was removed from Holy Cross on October 6, 2005. Affiant states that Thomas was ordered by the Diocese of Hamburg to leave all property belonging to the Parish at the church when Thomas left. Affiant states that the complainant, Kurry, informed him that when Thomas left the parish rectory he went to stay at the residence of a parish member and friend. This friend is a Jude Devlock. Devlock is a member of the Holy Cross Parish council and he is also a licensed attorney. Kurry stated that Thomas stayed with Devlock for a number of days in his Livingston County residence until Thomas left for a private residence in northern Michigan.

9. Affiant states that a check of Michigan Secretary of State records shows Jude Steven Devlock's address as

10. Affiant states that on October 18, 2005, he obtained consent from the Diocese and Holy Cross to search the rectory computer where the Child Sexually Abusive Material was observed. Affiant states that the computer was examined is a Gateway Computer, model number 300S, serial number 0029942615. Affiant states that this computer was examined by the MSP Computer Crimes Unit. Affiant states that the MSP Computer Crime unit found no evidence of any data on the hard drive of the computer. Affiant states that he was informed that this was unusual and the Computer Crime Unit had never previously encountered a computer hard drive with no data of any kind.

11. Affiant states he was contacted on November 15, 2005 by the complainant, Mark Kurry . Kurry stated that a meeting involving Father Wesley Thomas was held in Hamburg on November 10, 2005. Kurry stated that Jude Devlock accompanied Thomas to this meeting. Devlock told Kurry that he was there as a friend of Thomas' and was not representing him in any legal manner.

12. Kurry stated that during this meeting, Devlock stated that the hard drive from the computer that was in the rectory had been removed from the computer. This hard drive was removed prior to my seizing and searching the hard drive. Kurry informed me that Devlock admitted to currently possessing this hard drive.

D1547- Sea f
[Affiant, title & name]

Reviewed on:	Subscribed and sworn to before me on: 11/18/05
Date	Date
by:	Theresa M Brennan
Prosecuting Official	Judge/Magistrate

96

AFFIDAVIT FOR
SEARCH WARRANT

POLICE AGENCY
REPORT NUMBER:12-5383-05

13. Affiant states that he used the Gateway website to determine what hard drive was installed in the Gateway Computer, model number 300S, serial number 0029942615. According to Gateway, the hard drive installed in this computer was a Western Digital 40-GB 5M 40GPP Hard Disk Drive [Part #5502080].

14. Affiant states that the complainant Kurry informed me that no member of Diocese of Lansing or Holy Cross Church gave Devlock permission to remove or possess the computer hard drive. Kurry stated that the hard drive is the property of Holy Cross Church and the Diocese of Hamburg.

15. Affiant states that through his training and experience, persons keeping important items of a personal property tend to keep them in their residence, or in the case of a business owner, in businesses owned by them or in a place where their business is conducted.

16. Affiant states that probable cause exists that Jude Devlock is in possession of stolen property belonging to Holy Cross Church and the Diocese of Hamburg. Affiant further states that probable cause exists that the property to be searched for can be located in the locations described above.

17. Based on the above information, the Affiant respectfully requests this search warrant be granted for the items detailed above.

12-5383-05

DISGT. Se___

[Affiant, title & name]

Reviewed on:	Subscribed and sworn to before me on:
Date	11/13/05
	Date
by: _____	Theresa M Brennan
Prosecuting Official	Judge/~~Magistrate~~

97

The report reveals that a formal complaint was made to the Diocese of Hamburg and Bishop Martin by Alex's family regarding Father Thomas and the inappropriate relationship he was having with their teenage son. It is important to remember that when I brought my discovery to the attention of the Bishop, I was unaware of this formal complaint, but Bishop Martin was not. Yet, in an act of total negligence, he sent Father Thomas back to the parish regardless.

The report reveals that the hard drive of Father's computer was replaced with a brand new one. It also confirms that Jude Devlock not only helped Father replace the drive, he apparently kept the original drive hidden and remained silent while the police analyzed the wrong one. Further revealed is the fact that indeed search warrants were issued to retrieve the original drive from Devlock's possession. It is obvious that Devlock had no intentions of surrendering the drive until the authorities showed up at his door with the warrants.

The report reveals Father's intentions to erase the drive. It exposes Jude Devlock as a liar by contrasting his actual behavior against his own written account regarding these issues in his fax of January detailed in Chapter Seven.

The report details the involvement of an agent of Mother of God College in the continued mishandling and tampering of the evidence outside the knowledge of law enforcement authorities.

The report reveals that the Bishop indeed asked Father to return to active duty in his parish and get rid of the pornography on his computer.

The report reveals evidence of searches for child pornography and a fair amount of adult homosexual pornography.

Further confirmed is the fact that seven images of possible child pornography were discovered in a portion of the hard drive that rendered them un-prosecutable under Michigan law.

Documented in the report is the fact that Father Thomas had passwords established for the following three web sites: "boycherries.com," "twinks.com," and "1on1.militaryguy.com." One can only venture to guess that the passwords were something other than "holiness," his main Windows Operating System login password.

The report reveals that several of Father's emails referenced "teen" and or "young" pornography as well as emails referencing his membership on "boycherries.com."

The web cache internet history on Father Thomas' computer drive according to the police report contained web addresses with content relating to "teen," "boy," or "young" pornography. Also documented is evidence that Father's Yahoo and Google search history contained references to "teen" pornography.

Anyone who would deny behavioral impropriety after reading this report, and join Father in his denial would have to be mentally ill, simply unwilling to accept the truth about a troubled priest or as in the case of Devlock, willfully conspiring to protect a predator.

If the evidence in this case was not compromised concerning the potentially illegal images, and the State Police actually investigated boycherries.com and other sites for their content, it is reasonable to assume that Father Thomas would have been charged with felony possession of child pornography and use of a computer to commit a crime. Mr. Devlock would also have been charged with obstruction of justice for his role in hiding evidence, and possibly disbarred. As a result, I filed a formal complaint with the Attorney Grievance Commission of the Michigan State Bar regarding Devlock's abuse of his profession. The complaint was investigated by two members of the commission in Detroit and then suddenly and mysteriously halted. It was decreed by the commission that the case would be investigated no further. This is no surprise for many who have turned to the various attorney accountability boards across the country whose stated purpose is to supposedly keep watch on its own industry.

Chapter Nine
Warning Signs Overlooked

The benefit of hindsight at this juncture can put some things into perspective. Father's preoccupation despite warnings regarding Alex, the boy's presence at the rectory, and Father's almost daily involvement in the boy's life were very troubling indeed. Father's comments when speaking about Alex were often questionable. He mentioned that Alex was going to be his personal trainer using the new exercise machine he purchased for the rectory basement. Father mentioned to several people in the Parish that he may purchase a hot tub for his deck then commenting about having to be naked in the tub. Father asked a Parishioner to pray for him and Alex because he and the boy really loved each other and they were having difficulty with the boy's parents.

It certainly bears mentioning at this point that no evidence exists that the attraction Father had for Alex was mutual. It would appear that Father was grooming the boy without his knowledge. Alex apparently just took advantage of the attention, the affirmation, the understanding, and offers of refuge and gifts as any teenage boy might. Predators know the methodology of seduction and the vulnerability of children. Children in difficult family or social circumstances are in greater danger as the predator takes full advantage of the child's alienation. Priests who are also predators have a unique opportunity to molest in that they have access to many children, they have the trust of most adults and are privileged with personal information regarding family dynamics. This makes their actions so much more reprehensible.

One evening I was traveling back home with Father after we had both attended a conference. Father mentioned how disturbed he was whenever he thought about the notion of an adult molesting a minor, however he continued, "consensual behavior was an altogether different matter."

During a home school prom hosted at the Parish, Father was fascinated with two young men in particular. He asked those present repeatedly who they were and if any of us knew them. His attention remained fixed upon them throughout the evening. He was apparently unaware as to the appearance of his obvious interest in these boys.

On a continual basis, Father would express his intrigue concerning one or more of several teenage boys in the Parish. The comments were virtually always concerning how attractive and popular they were. I cannot remember one instance in which Father expressed such feelings toward one of the Parish girls. He was very insistent in his desire to have teenage boys doing odd jobs at the Parish and rectory both before and after Alex's time there.

On one occasion prior to my discovery, I was with Father at the rectory when a cable repairman and his son arrived to service the television. Oddly Father commented directly to the teenager regarding the boy's apparent Greek or Middle Eastern appearance. I remember thinking how strange that was.

Bring the Catholic chaplain at the local boy's juvenile prison, at one point, Father insisted that a newly released Hispanic boy accompany him and other members of the Parish on a mission trip to Mexico. Ultimately, Adam, the young man had to be transported home early due to his chronic misbehavior. It became obvious as time progressed that Father had a particular interest in young men of darker ethnic origin. Alex and Adam were Hispanic. The cable technician's son was darker in skin, and although no allegations of wrongdoing were ever asserted, Father did adopt an orphaned Palestinian teenage boy when he was in Israel many years prior.

Most curious was Father's apparent indifference toward the young ladies of the Parish. Unlike the boys, he virtually never mentioned them by name and never seemed to be really concerned with their struggles or situations. Additionally, and perhaps most significant was the fact that Father rarely mentioned his own mother. When he did it was only in passing and never in an endearing manner. Father was a single child and yet there were no photos or mementos of his parents in his residence or office. This fact gives rise to the notion that perhaps Father suffered some trauma or situation as a young man that may have indeed predisposed him to his disorder. This can be so very important in our understanding of how he may have suffered internally with this attraction and perhaps why he sought the priesthood as apparently so many other homosexual men did during the time of Father's ordination.

An indisputable aspect of Father's role as Pastor was his strange and often troubling treatment of women in general, most notably those on the office staff. Father's demeanor with them was often cold and disconnected. More than just occasionally he would become angry with them and unlike the male staff, would hold no reservations in openly expressing his outrage. I've seen him on occasion display nothing short of cruelty in his treatment of the ladies and I have never witnessed him issue an apology for it. During her brief two years of employment, one of our secretaries would be in my office regularly in tears regarding Father's attitude and treatment.

Another sign of trouble was Father's preoccupation with himself and his comforts. He shopped continuously. His groceries and household expenses were far beyond the reasonable level for a single man, especially one who should be accustomed to a certain level of austerity. He established a perpetual $10,000 annual budgetary figure for rectory improvements even though the Parish kept the house maintained, comfortable and functional.

On September 11, 2001, the staff as well as several Parishioners and indeed, most of the conscious world were fixed to the television in shock and horror. I recall Father called down from the rectory and was angry that someone must have used his carpet cleaning machine and left it in disrepair. Later on in the day, he expressed his dissatisfaction that the situation concerning his machine had still not yet been addressed. I remember thinking how can he possibly be thinking about this stupid appliance on this day when Western civilization was being attacked. I gave him the benefit of the doubt that he must have been so upset about the events of the day that he was purposely diverting his attention in an effort to deal with it.

Gradually, Father's ministry and role as Pastor began to suffer as well. My position as Business Manager was created to give the Pastor the opportunity to minister to his people without the burdens of Parish business. Almost immediately upon my arrival, however, Father began to disconnect from his Parish. As mentioned, he shopped a great deal during the day and often found other reasons to leave. His vacations and extended trips away from the Parish increased over the years. Expenses to bring priests in to offer Masses and other Sacraments eventually reached a critical level due to Father's increasing absence. Father expressed a frustration with the Parish schedule concerning confessions. He was chronically late to the confessional despite constant reminders which immensely frustrated our Parishioners. He became increasingly perturbed with Parishioners seeking him out and contacting him at home. He avoided real connection with Parishioners and volunteers and diverted all conflict, questions and controversy to my office.

Father's appreciation and attitude regarding holiness decreased dramatically while his concern with mere process and ritual increased. On one occasion, I remember Father's shocking indifference regarding an elderly Parishioner. The woman fell seriously ill and was rushed to the hospital. Her family asked Father to minister the last Sacraments to her. I offered to transport Father to the hospital. He refused. He said the last thing the medical staff needed was him in the way. Joe Lennon, then Deacon of the parish went to the hospital as soon as he found out that Father would not, but as a Deacon could not administer the Sacrament of the Sick. The Parishioner died soon after her arrival to the emergency room. The family was heartbroken at Father's lack of concern. The Deacon was beside himself regarding Father's growing lack of ministry concerning this instance and so many others. Deacon Joe's frustration had become a problem for Father. The deacon was preparing to approach the Bishop. Father was alerted to the deacon's plans and dismissed him on the spot.

It is important to understand, we are not mentioning Father's narcissism and inner struggles to berate or diminish his character. These things are noteworthy in this situation as indicators of

103

deeper internal issues. Preoccupation with self is common in men and women who suffer with same sex attraction. It has also been very common in the many clergy who have ultimately violated the trust of the innocent. Father was a man in need of help and as one of the severely troubled perpetrators of the church crisis was also abandoned by his own shepherds.

These were warning signs that isolated from each other and considered independently were rather easy to dismiss. Now that Father's problems had come to light, they form in retrospect, a dangerous mosaic poised to threaten the safety of the Parish youth.

Chapter Ten
Financial Transparency - The Red Herring

Not too far behind every allegation of sexual misconduct in any form you will most likely have the added complicated dimension of alleged financial foul play. This is the proverbial ancient axis of sex and money. It would seem as though you can't have the abuse of one without the other. Most of the cases of accused clergy in the global sex abuse crisis have been no exception. In these cases, broad allegations of embezzlement and misappropriation have been alleged. Of course in most every instance, the allegations of financial foul play have accompanied the sex charges against the priest or Bishop himself. In some others, the issue of illegal or immoral financial behavior was brought forth and levied against those who worked closely with the offending priest with his collaboration. Quite often though, as in our case, these allegations are levied against the whistleblower for the purpose of destroying credibility and redirecting the light of scrutiny away from the guilty. Remember if silence is the tool used by both corrupt church hierarchy and the guilty cleric's defenders, then something must be done about those who are determined to break the silence and tell the truth.

It is very important to consider that as soon as Father Klanyi arrived at Holy Cross, he ordered an audit of the Parish finances. The Diocese granted the audit in December of 2005. The independent auditor, Plante Moran although somewhat stunned at some of Father Thomas' spending habits, discovered absolutely no missing or misappropriated funds whatsoever. It is also very important to note that none of those who had joined Father Thomas in his dangerous denial were able to provide one piece of evidence to support their upcoming sinful accusations. But, as in so many cases, the gravity and damage are in the mere suggestion.

The financial dilemma as it pertains to Father Thomas took the form of reckless spending. The poor management of church resources by Father was an issue among many Parishioners and some were demanding reform for years prior to his removal. This financial discontent laid the foundation for Father Thomas' defenders upon his departure to immediately go to work to divert attention away from the troubled priest and his sins and attempt to thrust suspicion upon the church staff with me in the ultimate crosshairs.

Jude Devlock and Teresa Panky wasted no time in seizing the climate of financial discontent of the Parish and plotting their slanderous campaign toward me. Prior to the breaking news of Father's pornography addiction, neither Jude nor Teresa had any problem with the church finances. As a matter of fact, Devlock had the role as Father's "ombudsman" of interceding on behalf of legitimately concerned Parishioners and minimizing their financial worries. But all this was just too tempting for them to ignore as a vehicle for their sinful purposes. This was an opportunity to silence the truth about Father Thomas and punish me for tarnishing his reputation.

Now imagine the opportunity that a CPA and a lawyer with malevolent intentions would have to interject conflict and confusion in our finances. We already had a good deal of discontent among the Parishioners regarding Father Thomas' reckless spending, and we had our share of issues transitioning from many years using a homemade accounting program to the QuickBooks system, an industry standard. We had gone through three bookkeepers who had individually struggled with the new system's structure. This made our financial records vulnerable to Panky's manipulation. A CPA would have no problem keeping the level of confusion and suspicion above the heads of most members of the Finance and Parish Councils, and a lawyer skilled in language manipulation would have no problem crafting the verbiage of deceit. Our troubled CPA did have one significant obstacle, however. The Chair of the Finance Committee was a respectable and capable woman who understood the gravity of what Father Thomas had done and the outrageous campaign being sinfully wielded by his supporters. Mrs. Zelbeck's credentials were more accomplished, and she was smarter than Teresa Panky. She was of good will and emotionally stable. With an MBA in business and finance, being former acting Principal of the Parish school, and four years as Finance Chair, Judy was not easily fooled by Panky's bogus financial accusations. The problem remained, however that neither Judy nor I had any practical authority. We had to rely on Klanyi and the Diocese to control these nasty attackers which they were suspiciously unwilling to do. This sadly resulted in the agenda's uninterrupted progress.

In December of 2005, Father Thomas' supporters launched a tithing protest. They refused to financially support the Parish and actively tried to get others to join them. Their goal was twofold. First to have the whistleblower fired. Secondly, to have Father's name restored from shame to respect. The first facet of the plan was underway. They knew that a shortage of operating funds would only augment the frustrations of the Parishioners and increase the likelihood of a staff layoff.

Following Father Thomas' removal, Devlock and Panky interestingly and quite suddenly developed deep concerns regarding the Parish's finances. Allegations began to emanate from both of them that I was hiding financial transactions and failing to properly report the church's fiscal activity. It did not matter that these vicious allegations bore no basis in truth and defied actual evidence to the contrary. During our budget preparation in the summer of 2006, someone leaked a confidential copy of our budget draft to Panky. The woman boldly migrated the draft into her own computer, manipulated the file and then sent it out to the whole Parish Council with her disparaging remarks and accusations of mishandling. A Parishioner told me that he had overheard Teresa Panky telling another that she and her husband were scouring the internet attempting to find something they could use to damage my credibility. During the same time, Devlock, a current member of the Council went so far as to commit libel in a written statement he made to the Parish Council concerning The Holy Cross Development Association, an independent non-profit community organization and my office's handling of Parish funds: His outrageous statement verbatim:

"Substantial Parish funds were thereafter transferred into this entity."

It is bound to give one pause when a lawyer, an active member of the Parish, whom everyone seemed to trust, accuses someone of committing a felony. Devlock knew this. He also knew that as the "ombudsman" whom I worked with on many occasions, that this accusation he maliciously levied against me was absolutely false. When you consider Devlock's behavior laced throughout the State Police report, and the Father Lindst incident, however, no one should be surprised that he would lie again to the Parish Council to keep the truth concealed about Father Thomas.

Immediately following this sinful attack on my character, I contacted the Diocese of Hamburg and demanded their intervention. They had a duty to prevent harassment in the workplace and respond to this. The appeal:

May 17, 2006

Deacon Mark Kurry
Diocese of Hamburg

Dear Mark,

Thank you for taking my call this morning. As we discussed, I am practicing a level of patience that is not easy amidst this open and vicious harassment from Jude Devlock, a member of the Pastoral Council of Holy Cross Church. He is using this platform of the Pastoral Council to endlessly conduct his attacks. Devlock is also on the Cemetery Board of this Parish and a Religious Education Catechist. To a lesser degree, Teresa Panky, working closely with him has also assisted in causing discord, doubt and suspicion in our fractured Parish.

Devlock's latest writing via email that you have in your possession contains blatant libel against my character and reputation. I am understandably approaching the limit of my passive endurance. I have every right both canonically and civilly to protect my good name from attack.

I am again appealing to Holy Cross Parish and the Diocese of Hamburg to intervene. It is the responsibility of my employer to address harassment that occurs in the workplace. Although it is true that Mr. Devlock is not an employee, he does serve as a volunteer in the Parish and his position has apparent authority to our Parishioners. I contend that his position does indeed afford to him the ability to effectively harass me and other members of the staff and volunteers.

As I mentioned in my original correspondence in having to report the tragic misdeeds of our pastor, I need the Diocese to protect my job. In return for my salary, I have always and will continue to offer honest and diligent service to my church in the presence of my God. My efforts in bringing the actions of Father Thomas to the attention of the Diocese was part of that service and regrettably has become the fuel for the plots of ill-intentioned aggressors.

Thank you very much. God bless you.

Patrick J. Flynn, Business Manager

.cc Father Steve Klanyi
.cc Msgr. Michael Mira
.cc Msgr. Steven Benke
.cc Bishop Carl F. Martin

The response of the Bishop and the Diocese was silence. They refused to intervene. Sadly, this weakness and abdication of sacred duty is precisely why the global catastrophe in the church occurred and why it continues to this day.

We then received a fax at the Parish office. Devlock was resigning from the Parish Council and leaving the Parish. Later that day, Mark Kurry called me from the Diocese to offer excuses as to why they would do nothing concerning this lying attorney. I told Kurry of Devlock's departure. Kurry seemed surprised and alluded that he did not know about it. At any rate, Devlock's physical presence left the church, but he remained well involved behind the scenes in lock step with Mrs. Panky.

At this point, Father Thomas' team of conspirators seemed to add a new member to its ranks. Our new Deacon, Jack Boehman apparently joined Panky in her work. Jack was appointed by Father Thomas before he was removed and despite the evidence in the State Police report, the new Deacon simply refused to believe the truth about his priest. In Parish Council meetings, the Deacon was determined to exaggerate the audit report from Plante Moran.

He asserted that the recommendation for the strengthening of internal controls was a dire indication of financial foul play. We now had a member of the clergy in our Parish determined to keep suspicion at a heightened level against the Finance Committee and the Business Manager's office. The Deacon had formal responsibilities as a clergy member of the Parish Council. He neglected those responsibilities during this time and seemed to fix his attention and efforts on fostering fables of financial suspicion. According to an eyewitness, the deacon recommended to Father Klanyi that a warning be placed in my personnel file in response to the Plante Moran audit.

In November of 2005, the Finance Office of the Hamburg Diocese issued the letter scheduling the Plante Moran audit. In the brief announcement was a directive to inform a certain Parishioner, a CPA (Mrs. Panky) who was involving herself with Parish finances to please withdraw from that involvement. I wanted to produce the letter the Diocese issued but I accidentally misplaced it. I asked Father Klanyi if he had a copy. He said that he vaguely remembered such a letter but did not have it.

I then called the office of Finance at the Diocese and asked them if they could run me another copy of the letter. I informed them that we were beginning to have trouble with the CPA and her refusal to back off. Surprisingly, the Finance Office denied knowledge of ever issuing such a letter. I asked them to search their correspondence records for November of 2005. They called me back and said they found no such letter and reiterated that they did not know what I was referring to. I knew that the Diocese keeps thorough records of all correspondence. This was a serious red flag that began to reveal the Diocese of Hamburg was interested in something other than the truth and the healing of our Parish. As time progressed, it became more and more obvious I was right in suspecting their efforts to silence this tragedy thereby lending their approval and assistance to great sinners in the Parish.

I redoubled my efforts to scour my files and finally found the letter that had so conveniently vanished from the memory of the Diocese.

CATHOLIC DIOCESE OF HAMBURG

November 21, 2005

Rev. Steven Klanyi
Holy Cross Parish

Dear Fr. Klanyi:

This is to confirm our phone conversation that the Diocese conducts a Parish audit of Holy Cross Parish. The Diocese contracts with Plant-e Moran to conduct these engagements, therefore a representative of the firm will contact the Parish in the near future to arrange dates for their visit.

The focus of a Parish audit is on the internal controls that are functioning at the Parish and evaluating those controls in accordance with the stated policies and procedures in the Diocesan Internal Controls and Accounting Manual. The staff of Plante Moran is very familiar with the Diocesan expectations and Parish structure having conducted these audits for a number of years. The result of the Diocesan process will be a written report that identifies concerns and the actions that need to be taken.

It is our understanding that a local CPA, a Parishioner, has been conducting some reviews of Parish financial activity. In light of the Diocesan audit there is no reason for this person to continue their activity.

Sincerely,

Thomas G. Pastine
Finance Officer

There it is signed by Tom Pastine, the Diocesan Financial Officer himself. In spite of the letter's existence, Panky did not retreat from her involvement and, of course, the Diocese and our cowardly priest were not going to do anything about it. As a matter of fact, Teresa vied for an opening on the Parish Council and no doubt was overjoyed to find her name was randomly selected at the drawing to fill the empty seat. Now the tremendous opportunity to work her agenda was in place. In the months that ensued, Mrs. Panky hijacked virtually every Parish Council meeting with filibustering banter, controversy and conflict absolutely preventing the council's business from rising above her invented financial scandal.

The next item on the red herring agenda was to call for an historical comparison of the Parish finances over the previous five years. Lengthy council arguments eventually settled on a consensus to produce a three-year history. The report was prepared by the Finance Council and presented to father Klanyi for approval. Upon pastoral approval, the report was issued to the Parish Council. Panky immediately led an effort to reject the report as completely inadequate and resumed her incessant call for financial transparency. She was able to muster some additional support from other Council members along with Deacon Boehman and others who refused to accept the truth about Father Thomas and wanted to see me punished for exposing him. Later on that week, Panky emailed the Parish Council and told them what she expected to see in the form of a report. As a sample of what she expected, she attached a fifty-five page five-year exhaustive financial report from General Motors. One would have wondered at this move if the woman was even stable enough to be responsible for her own actions. Father Klanyi during a rare moment of tongue-in-cheek levity commented that we will most likely find her one day lying in a fetal position in the corner sucking her thumb. It's amazing that a man could express his opinion in that manner and yet then succumb to the woman's every unreasonable rant permitting her to seriously damage the Parish community under his watch. That calls for a level of integrity that drops below the meter for any leader. It is an abdication I simply will never understand.

We appealed to Father Klanyi to end this ridiculous fiasco in reminding him that he himself, as pastoral authority of the Parish, approved the submitted three-year historical report. Father in his unbelievable weakness refused to lead. This was empowering to Panky for her to continue her agenda of defamation and the trouble only progressed as she persisted in accusing me and the Finance Committee of still hiding the financials.

The next demand from our troubled CPA and those who would conceal the actions of a predator was for my office to produce each month extensive varying financial reports to the Parish Council. Included in these reports were to be rolling profit and loss statements. This was far above and beyond the practice of any other church in the region. I looked to Father Klanyi for reasonable intervention. When was I going to learn my lesson in that regard? Father was incapable of leadership and absolutely feared these bullies. So, I produced a prototype of the reports and submitted them to Father for approval during the Finance Council meeting. Once again, Father approved the reports only to buckle under the pressure again when predictably, they were rejected by the scandal makers at the next meeting of the Parish Council.

In an effort to go the extra mile and hopefully buy some peace for the Parish, my office along with the Finance Committee went above and beyond in providing financial documentation. We also made every aspect of the Parish finances available to any Parishioner who inquired. All they had to do was ask.

Of course this thorough and painstaking financial transparency did not satisfy the accusers. Quite simply, that's because financial transparency, despite their incessant demand for it, was not their goal. Their goal was to create sufficient scandal to exonerate Father Thomas by default through discrediting his whistleblower.

This was beyond an example of workplace harassment. It could be more accurately described as occupational terrorism as my character, reputation and ability was relentlessly and sinfully attacked under both the watch and passive approval of Klanyi and the Diocese.

Once again, I appealed to the Diocese for their intervention. This is not because I expected them to care or to act appropriately. At this juncture, I knew better than to expect justice. This appeal and all subsequent appeals were issued to create a paper trail detailing my deferral to authority, my employer's failure to help me, and their intent to remain silent regarding the potential violation of innocent children. I was indeed a marked man. All indications suggested the Diocese, Klanyi and the scandal makers at the church were operating in some variety of collaborative understanding with each other.

Chapter Eleven

Kill the Messenger

Simple logic dictated that Klanyi and the Diocese had within their authority the ability and duty to bring healing to our church and justice to those injured by the scandal. Their own sexual misconduct policies and procedures mandated appropriate response. At best, they simply didn't care. At worst, they were determined to sanitize their reputations and destroy the credibility of the victims.

This campaign of harassment involved both the tag-teaming of several people in their attack on the whistleblower and church leadership's failure to intervene for eighteen months. Under most circumstances, the whistleblower would buckle under the pressure and resign to escape the suffering. I'm convinced this was the hope of Father Thomas, his defenders, Klanyi and the Diocese. I believe they were supremely frustrated with my endurance. It seemed that they needed to step up their efforts if they ever were to accomplish their goal. Incidentally, this goal and all efforts undertaken to achieve it are criminal. *Constructive Discharge* is the term for making the working conditions intolerable for those who report wrongdoing in the workplace. Its intended goal is the resignation of the whistleblower. It is a crime under federal and state law and the criminals in this story are Church leaders.

Despite the lack of basis in fact and even evidence to the contrary, financial mishandling remained the constant cry of the cover up brokers. Normal Parish business and progress were impossible as their filibuster paralyzed every Parish Council meeting.

Nevertheless, parish operations needed to continue in the midst of this agenda. During this time, the church exterior was in desperate need of new paint. I got Father Klanyi directly involved with other staff members and volunteers to select a new color for the building. Father chose a color theme that was a refreshing change from the original beige paint. The staff and volunteers approved and we contracted a painting firm to do the job.

This was an opportunity for Father Bill's defenders to once again attack me professionally. They all decided they hated the new color once they found out I was involved in the repainting. They blamed me exclusively and expressed their outrage giving the illusion that they really cared about such things. Even though they had all stopped their own financial support of the parish, they boldly demanded the church spend another $14,000 to change the color. They had hoped that this wasting of the parish funds would be the final blow to the whistleblower.

I reminded the parish who these people were, the apologists of a predator, what they were really trying to do and the fact that the man placed in charge of the parish by the Diocese was the one who selected the color. In his unrelenting weakness, Father Klanyi actually considered giving in to their demands until the staff and parishioners of good will protested. So, because Father was even too weak to do the wrong thing, the church still bears the new color.

During the unfolding of this fiasco at one of the Parish Council meetings, the Parish Youth Director presented a letter written by my 17 year-old daughter, Lily. In the letter, she expressed the damage the youth of the Parish were enduring over the hatred and contention caused by Father Bill's supporters. The adult parishioners had a moral obligation before God to set a holy example for the children. However, a horrible witness was being given to these young Christians whose faith was new and understandably vulnerable. The letter contained an appeal for these people to please think about the effects of their efforts and stop their attacks at once. Because the author was my daughter, the letter was quickly dismissed and its urgent message ignored by the scandal makers present. Subsequently, a large majority of the Parish's young people who watched this unfold have since left Holy Cross.

The protectors of a predator, the brokers of unholy silence and outright character assassins were undaunted by this latest failure to ruin my career. They wasted no time in rolling up their sleeves and getting back to work to kill the messenger. Their new tactic had to be substantial and had to cause immense damage to my credibility if they were ever to advance their agenda. With the help of a new recruit named Mike Klyde, they quickly went to work. One morning, Klyde emailed me asking if I could provide for him the details of our special water assessment tax for the Parish campus. The $200,000 assessment was a huge financial burden to the Parish and seemed to be volatile enough of an issue to use to try to attack my professional position in the Parish.

I took great care to inform Klyde of every detail as to the nature of the assessment, the mandatory obligation it represented and the scope of principal and interest payable each year for the next eighteen years.

Klyde, working directly with Teresa Panky contacted Father Thomas at his cottage and devised a plan. Teresa contacted the Supervisor's office at Green Oak Township and misrepresented herself as having the authority to act on behalf of the Parish to seek information. Panky then misrepresented the facts concerning the assessment in a written document. The document falsely stated that our Parish was strapped with this overwhelming assessment due to my negligence. Klyde wasted no time in presenting the fraudulent document to Father Klanyi. The false statement verbatim:

> "Pat Flynn was to attend the public hearing about 18 months ago, and offer an objection to the 30 water taps in question and the township would have honored the request. According to Mark St. Charles, Pat Flynn DID attend the public hearing, but DID NOT make an objection, so the 30 water tap assessment was not changed."

Father brought the document to me the next day and asked me about the situation considering the fact that he was not at the Parish when the assessment was established. I explained the truth to him and tried to make him understand that this was yet another attempt to draw attention away from Father Thomas and to discredit me. I asked him to consider the sheer absurdity of two people who no longer contribute to the support of the church attempting to appear so concerned as to one of its debts. Father mentioned that we would have to consult with the township to get to the bottom of this. I was insulted that Father Klanyi was entertaining as even remotely credible the accusations of these proven troublemakers. I issued the following letter to Fr. Klanyi in response:

February 3, 2007

Father Steve Klanyi
Canonical Administrator
Holy Cross Roman Catholic Church

Dear Father,

I have been searching my heart in prayer to write this letter. No one is being copied on this. It is between you and me. You met with Mike Klyde yesterday with a warning in your heart. I alerted you to the newest effort on behalf of Klyde and Mrs. Panky to discredit me and to further damage our suffering and bleeding Parish. Since neither of them care about the church as evidenced by their theft of God's resources (the withholding of any offering), their plans could not have been clearer to you. You gave them an undeserved voice and entertained with seriousness the details of their sinful, malicious, defaming act.

You told me that you now have to go to the Township to learn the truth. You couldn't have hurt me more than if you stabbed me. I am not in the least wary of the way in which I performed my duties in regard to the special tax assessment. I am secure in the knowledge that the way in which I dispensed my duties and in the extensive discourse with our local government, I have witnessed well for our Parish and for Jesus Christ.

What hurts, Father, is that you even feel the impulse to go and verify. In the sixteen months since your arrival, I have been a good servant to you and this Parish. I have exercised virtue in my service during this catastrophe. Likewise, during that same sixteen months, you have witnessed Teresa Panky do nothing but attack, belittle and cause conflict and confusion. Yet, you put this latest appalling presentation of hers on a level playing field with my word and proven dedication. This is most hurtful and so very wrong. That being said, I am not deterring you from going to the Township if you want to do that.

You have rightly identified a troubling element of self-righteousness in our Parish. Mrs. Panky and Mike Klyde, like

118

Jude Devlock before them are hell-bent on hiding the truth and vilifying anyone who would bring it to light even to the extent of illegally harassing a whistleblower. Father, their behavior is a hell of a lot worse than self-righteousness. It's worse because the protection of the innocent is at stake. Well, Father, like it or not, God has positioned you to finally do something about it. You didn't ask for this, I know that and I truly feel your pain. But you see, we have something in common. My cross is no night at the opera either, Father. And just like you, I didn't ask for this. It has been 34 months since this cross was handed to me. The time for placating, and passivity is over. God is not asking me to respond to this shameful attack on my family and livelihood with weakness. The rubber has hit the proverbial road.

If you do not act immediately to remove Mrs. Panky and Mr. Klyde from their respective places of honor and influence on the Parish and Finance Councils, you will be abdicating your duty as temporary shepherd. You must stop the bleeding in this church. I think that you really want to and I pray with all my heart that you do. If you ignore this, you will have God to answer to for permitting his Parish to be destroyed. Likewise, ignoring this will force me to take matters into my own hands. I don't want to do that, Father. I'm damn tired of fighting. Please don't underestimate my resolve, however, if need be. I did not walk through this raging fire only to watch our Parish go down at the hands of liars and perverts.

You know it is not my character to approach authority figures like this. I am neither a difficult person nor a malcontent. My nature is both pleasant and efficient. I have great respect for structure and authority and I strive to be the best example to my seven children. I hate that I have to use such strong words. I have been compelled to do so from deep within my heart after years of failing passivity and unjust humiliation. You sat in a meeting not too long ago where the attendees affirmed to you the campaign afoot to drive me from my position on the staff. With this knowledge, you have the obligation to address it. You are not legally permitted to continue to allow this occupational harassment under the recently enacted Whistleblower Protection Acts embedded in both Michigan and Federal law. You are not free to watch these ill-intentioned individuals damage my career and my family with their hatred.

I'm not scolding you. I am appealing to you. I cannot fight this injustice alone. Please Father, help me. Help your Parish. Help the God to whom you have given your life, to effect justice and courageous stewardship upon this suffering community. I pledge continued faithful service to you, but I desperately need your leadership. God be with you and with our Parish.

Patrick

We scheduled a meeting with the township supervisor and received the following letter in my support:

GREEN OAK CHARTER TOWNSHIP
10001 SILVER LAKE ROAD
BRIGHTON, MICHIGAN 48116

February 12, 2007

Patrick Flynn
Business Manager
Holy Cross Catholic Church
P.O. Box 610 Hamburg, M1 48139-0610

Re: Water Taps

Dear Patrick,

First I wish to thank you for providing the Township with the official letter outlining the spokesperson for Holy Cross Church. This will in the future assist us in working together on projects such as utilities in the area.

Also I wish to acknowledge your January 30, 2007 correspondence regarding the reduction of water service taps from the current 35 to 17. Further I feel obligated to note that on two other occasions (March 11, 2005 & October 26, 2005) your office sent correspondence noting the churches desire to reduce the 35 taps. These two correspondences were based on a meeting that we had in which I recall Father Thomas was present.

I also wish to acknowledge the correspondence that is being circulated by Mrs. Panky in which she outlines a conversation that she and I had. Mrs. Panky called our Treasurers office and my deputy's office, when I returned her call, **Mrs. Panky represented herself as one having authority to speak on behalf of the church.** Mrs. Panky and I discussed how the taps were arrived at and the possibility of divesting of the taps. **Mrs. Panky stated that she had authority to discuss the removal**

of all thirty five taps and I responded to her that prior to me finding a potential purchaser for the taps, that I would have to have a letter or authorization in writing from the church. Mrs. Panky has made some statements that may have been taken out of content or misunderstood so therefore I now wish to review history on the entire water tap issue.

In or about 2003, the Township was in the process of establishing a water system within Green Oak Township. The water line began at the Green Oak Township northern border with the Charter Township of Brighton and proceeded south along VS 23, along Rickett Road, west along Winans, South along Musch and eventually ended at Spicer Road and M-36. This route was directly in front of Holy Cross Church on two sides. Knowing that the church had some plans for a school, I made an appointment to meet with Father Thomas, and yourself in which we discussed the church's future plans. When we met, you provided me with a set of plans that I took to our engineers for a review to determine the total taps needed at the time for your school. Based on the engineers review of class rooms and square footage, it was determined that based on our approved residential equivalent units (R.E.IJ.) you would need 35 taps.

We relayed this information to you and proceeded with the SAD. This was primarily due to the future plans that the church had at that time. The public hearings were held under Public Act 188 and the Special assessment district (SAD) was approved.

There was no objection due to the fact that at that time as even we understood it, you still planned the school that was shown in the plans presented to me at our meeting.

As the economy started to downturn at the end of 2004 and into 2005, we were notified by Holy Cross Church that the church was down sizing its plans for the school. As I explained to you at that time, we could not reduce the SAD once it had been approved. Further I explained that it would be possible (but difficult) to sell or redistribute the taps.

In Mrs. Panky's memo the statement that I believe was misunderstood is that the discussion of the downsized school came after the SAD was approved and not before. **Also as I had mentioned to Mrs. Panky that the reason Mr. Flynn was at the public hearing and offered no objection is due to the fact that at the time of the hearing, the full size school was still in the plans.**

121

Current status: The problem that we have been faced with is how to reduce the number of taps. We have been looking for a user who is willing to purchase the taps. We have been looking for someone who will purchase the taps at face value. At face value we then could use some of the funds to pay off the remaining debt on the taps and refund the Church their out of pocket expense, minus interest. As one may guess, we have not been successful. First, this is primarily due to the fact that we have not had anyone until recently purchasing taps. Secondly, most users of the water system up to this point have preferred to be included in a SAD where they can spread the cost of the taps over twenty years. Third, is that if we were to just transfer the unpaid debt to another user, we can only do so if the property owner that we will transfer the SAO to was in the original district that the taps came from. We have not had anyone wishing more taps; we do have the possibility of such a sale. Just for the record, I will try to get the church some or the entire amount of out of pocket funds minus the interest but I will not make any promises. We have no mechanism to force a purchaser to pay the out of pocket expenses that the church has acquired.

Please be advised that as far the SAD and the water taps, **the Church and the Township worked together within the law and in everyone's best interest. To state otherwise is a misrepresentation of the facts.**

Please let it be known that it is the position of the Township to honor the churches wishes to reduce the total taps to 17 within the boundaries that we are allowed to do so. The Township respects the Churches management and will not be caught up in the struggles that are currently occurring within the Church. Other than the normal information that is freely public information, we will only discuss disposition of utilities with representatives designated officially by the Church.

I sincerely hope that this letter helps in clarifying the issues.

Most Sincerely,
Mark St.Charles, Supervisor
Cc: Township Board Members Thomas Connelly, Township Attorney

There was no apology from Panky or Klyde, no remorse, not even a hint of acknowledgement that what was presented to Klanyi was proven to be false or grossly misunderstood. The truth of course is there was no misunderstanding. There was only the effort to defame. With their most blatant attack backfiring and subsequently exposed for its malice, I once again appealed to both my pastor and the Diocese of Hamburg for intervention. I sought as a matter of complete propriety and good business practices the removal of these individuals from their places on the Parish Council and the Finance Committee for what they had attempted. I was ignored again. Father Klanyi told me that the Diocese informed him that he could do what he wanted but that they saw no reason for him to do anything. So once again, the Diocese of Hamburg and Bishop Martin would fail to exercise their duty to protect Christ's Church. Since Father Klanyi was already accustomed to indifference and weakness this was of course a no-brainer message of relief for him. One could legitimately wonder if they possibly could have been more obvious that they supported the agenda to silence the truth.

I issued another appeal to the Diocese which generated absolutely no response:

February 2, 2007

Deacon Mark Kurry
Diocese of Hamburg

Dear Mark,

Mike Klyde met with Father Steve this past Friday morning and presented a defaming document to him that was written by Teresa Panky. Klyde relayed to Father that he even contacted Father Thomas by phone regarding the information in the document. This is outrageous! The document falsely and shockingly asserts that I have cost this Parish tens of thousands of dollars and that ten times that amount would have been lost in the coming 17 years.

We now find ourselves at the same point we were when Jude Devlock distributed libelous statements against me in Parish Council. This Parish and the Diocese of Hamburg cannot and must not permit this harassment against my character and my dignity as a faithful employee of the Church. Both have a legal and moral obligation to step in and stop this sinful effort.

Father Steve presided over a meeting called by several members of the Parish Council about 9 months ago. One of the attendees told me in that meeting Father Steve asked those present if they felt there was an effort afoot to run me out of the Parish. They all concurred that there was. There is absolutely no confusion concerning Teresa Panky's intentions and efforts in this clear agenda against me as a whistleblower.

Teresa Panky currently serves on the Parish Council. Mike Klyde currently serves on the Finance Council, is president of the School Advisory Board, and represents the School Principal on the Parish Council. These positions afford them the ability to effect significant harassment and defamation intended to seriously damage my career, solid reputation and family welfare. Unbelievably, they conduct their campaign while refusing any support to their Parish from their personal resources. The notion that they care about their church is therefore, absurd. I expect these ill-intentioned individuals to be removed from their respective positions immediately. I have no problem with their continued presence as Parishioners. Direct action by those in authority now will send a powerful message to any who have it in their will to abuse our Parish and affect its continued suffering. Doing nothing now will accomplish the opposite, and the bleeding will continue. Likewise, as long as Wesley Thomas has their ears and is permitted to interfere with our Parish's healing, we will still have to deal with this "insurgency" to some degree. That is a matter for the higher church authority to deal with. We pray for a solution to this problem soon.

I am no longer content with passivity watching this hateful cancer consume this Parish. I am demanding that action be taken immediately. It is clear what needs to be done. I suppose the question remains will those who hold authority do the right thing. You cannot imagine how I pray that they do.

Thank you very much. God bless you.

Patrick J. Flynn
Business Manager

.cc Father Steve Klanyi
    Judy Zelbeck

Joseph Bartram
Anna Peloni
Robert Delisi

* According to the Offering module of our Parish database which is meticulously maintained in compliance with ICAM published by the Diocese.

With the apparent approval of the Bishop and the Diocese, the whining and bogus cries of financial misconduct continued to dominate business in the Parish Council as Father Klanyi sat in complete resignation and abdication of his duty. I had decided the time had arrived to truly pull the curtain back on this malicious agenda. Since transparency seemed to be the ceaseless belching from malicious council members, I was determined to give them a dose of financial transparency they would not soon forget. It was daunting to consider that I would have to act unilaterally considering I was getting no support from any authority whatsoever.

As a member of the Parish Council by virtue of my position on the church staff, it was my duty to issue a report each month on the Parish finances. Following was my report issued to the Parish Council at its April 2007 meeting:

Patrick J. Flynn
Ministry Report April 19, 2007

Investments and Savings
$70,822 - Bequest and Building Fund
$37,620 - Diocesan Savings Account

Financial "Transparency":

Once again last meeting, Mrs. Panky with promised support from Mike Klyde has succeeded in resurrecting endless banter regarding our past financial reports. Their continued badgering is no less than shocking considering their fraudulent handling of the water assessment in an effort to assault my character and damage me professionally. Mrs. Panky is a tithing protester for 12 months running now. She has the gall to ask us to believe she cares about her Parish's finances and demand exhaustive historical "digging." This seems odd since the time frame that they are focusing on was filled with Father Thomas' reckless

125

financial management and violation of Diocesan policy. She didn't have a problem then. She was silent as the grave. Actually, her suspicions did not curiously arise until after Father's removal. Please see attached file, Diocese 1. The Diocese asked that Mrs. Panky withdraw from the finances since very competent authority was at work taking care of our Parish. Apparently, she has the same problem with obedience that she does with charity and propriety. The Diocesan auditor, Plante-Moran is satisfied with our financial history. The bi-council audit compliance oversight team is satisfied with our financial history. All Parishioners of good will are satisfied. But, these individuals are not. If anyone has merited suspicion, it should be them.

Fair, enough. Since financial "Transparency" in our current time when all financial processes are responsible and free of error do not seem to interest the few scandal makers among us, and we seem for whatever reason, unable to move on, we will begin pulling back the curtain on that time period they allude to and shine a bright light. Don't be surprised though if it ends up being more than anyone bargained for concerning Father Thomas' leadership. I was hoping we could have moved on without having to reveal this. After all, was it not already done and in the past? Could any of it be undone? No one can deny that I have been reserved for all this time concerning Father Thomas' financial handling. I have been pushed to this point.

Do you think that I am sounding defensive? I'll ask you to put yourself in my place and consider how patient I really have been. It has been 18 months of this endless, un-Christian defamation. 18 months of unjust and unwarranted suffering for my family. During that time the Parish Council has been paralyzed by this ugly agenda first launched by Jude Devlock (currently under investigation by the Michigan State Bar). The agenda is simply this:

"To divert the focus and light of truth away from Father Thomas concerning the condition of the Parish and to create scandal against his whistleblower."

The fact is Father Thomas is in desperate need of help. He is addicted to youth homosexual pornography. That's the truth substantiated by the Michigan State Police investigation. Please deal with it. He is in personal denial and is being enabled by a small group of supporters. I am the target of their hatred because I have had the difficult, devastating, and heart-wrenching obligation of having had to report him to church authorities.

Are you all sick of this crap? God knows I am. The agenda by the scandal makers and the tithing protesters had damaged our Parish considerably. What will your reaction as a council be? Are you content with the status quo? The difficult question that must be asked is, are any of you actually enjoying this drama? I hope you're not. You should be ashamed of yourself if you are. This is God's house.

It is important to state that there is no evidence that Father Thomas set out to maliciously waste Parish resources. Nevertheless, this was the essence of all Parish frustration with our finances and the reason for the top priority at our Summit during the time prior to October, 2005.

Father Thomas authorized the pay out of over $ 170,000 in Parish assets for his failed $60 million dollar campus building idea. This included $28,000 to pay four architects to merely bid on the job. I vehemently protested this to no avail. When the project manager began invoicing the Parish $9400 each month, Father refused to fire him. Fr. Bill ended up paying this man $72,225. I am the one who stopped this disaster and prompted the Parish Council, Finance Council, and the Building Committee to force Father's hand to end this fiasco. The cost still goes on for our Parish in the form of a utility assessment that is twice its reasonable amount adding another $37,000.00 to the loss to date and counting.

In the four categories of personal spending including clergy extra help, groceries and entertainment, mileage, and rectory enhancements, our current priest has spent an annual $4037 as opposed to Father Thomas' annual average of $32,150.

Father Thomas installed a chain-link fence for his dogs when he arrived in 1999, only to replace it in 2004 with an expensive wooden fence.

Father Thomas, in violation of Diocesan policy, took a personal loan from the Parish for $8300 for his cottage and waited for 18 months to replace the money without any interest.

Father Thomas took another personal loan from the Parish for $815 in 2005 for his car. He refuses to pay it back despite numerous invoices and statements I have issued to collect.

Father Thomas offered a loan for $1800 from Parish resources to a Parishioner.

Father Thomas established a $40,000 annual staff position for the primary purpose of raising funds. He promised to keep that position contingent on performance. He broke his promise to the Parish in this regard.

Father Thomas bought an $80,000 electronic organ after only ten percent of the Parish said they wanted it and only three percent said they would financially support its purchase. Father tried to hide the down payment on the instrument as a "consulting" fee, but then relented when I warned him against it.
Acting School Principal, Judy Zelbeck presented a $60,000 budget deficit for the school which Father Thomas vehemently refused to disclose to the Parish. As a result that year, the Finance Council refused to approve the Parish budget. The Parish Council condemned this failure of disclosure.

Father used church resources to supply a cell phone to the boy who worked for him at the rectory.

More to come next meeting.

World War III erupted as Father Thomas' team led by our deacon attempted to silence this disclosure. Deacon Jack called for an immediate renunciation of my report and to have it stricken from official Parish records. His motion was put to a vote and failed to pass.

This development presented a great dilemma for Father Thomas, his supporters, Father Klanyi, and Bishop Martin. It was now quite obvious that silence would be broken despite their best efforts and the truth concerning a predator and church leadership's determination to protect him was going to be revealed.

Apparently the need for damage control would be the suspicious motivator for swift Diocesan action. The very next day, the Bishop issued a decree dissolving both the Parish Council and the Finance Council at Holy Cross. It is nothing short of amazing how quickly they really can respond when they want to.

In a desperate and disgraceful attempt to re-establish the controlled atmosphere of silence, I believe Father Klanyi, Deacon Boehman,

Mark Kurry, Bishop Martin, and Monsignor Mira convened prior to this action.

On May 29, 2007 after I returned from a family vacation, I was called into Father Klanyi's office and there both Klanyi and Boehman dissolved my position on the Parish staff. The firing was disguised as a layoff for financial reasons. I was told to proceed directly to the parking lot and others would be appointed to gather my personal belongings. Before leaving, however, I was presented with a rather interesting proposal and three weeks with which to ponder it.

The proposal was basically an insurance policy for the Diocese, the Parish, Father Thomas, all of his supporters, and Father Klanyi to be able to rebuild their infrastructure of silence and cover up. This insurance plan was devised to prevent vehicles of truth such as this book from being established. The proposal also demanded the terms and conditions of the proposal itself remain hidden (protected by silence). The Diocese in its cunning way felt sure I would sign this deal because it came with $18,000 of continued paychecks for me, 4 months of healthcare for my family, and a much needed letter of recommendation from Klanyi. The proposal also mentioned that I must acquit and discharge all claims, known and unknown against among others, **volunteers** or **council members**. Isn't that curious? Why would the church wish to legally cover for the personal actions of volunteers unless they were involved in the direction of their efforts?

The Diocese was wrong to assume that I would accept hush money in exchange for my silence. They must have arrogantly surmised that I would be willing to sell my principles and personal moral dignity for a fair sum. At the end of the three week period, I issued the following letter to Klanyi and copied it to the other notables:

June 14, 2007

Father Steven Klanyi
Holy Cross Roman Catholic Church

Dear Father,

As you know you terminated my position on the afternoon of May 29. You have stated in writing that reason for this termination was for purely budgetary purposes.

When my position was created in 2000, there was great purpose for it. Father Thomas convinced the Parish Council and the Administrative Committee that this position would remove the burdens of business details from the shoulders of the pastor allowing him to shepherd his flock and evangelize full time. Indeed the training of a priest greatly involves pastoral care in tending souls and growing the flock of Christ's Church.

It was Father Thomas' obligation to the Parish to be this shepherd. It was his obligation to be responsible, compassionate, and to witness God's love. Instead, he used my position as an excuse to disappear. He was unreachable to a good portion of his Parish. He distanced and isolated himself. He was reckless and selfish with Parish resources. His demeanor and character deteriorated over the years and this drove more than just a few people away rather than toward our Parish. Then of course, it became obvious that he was doing the unthinkable, and apparently, the unspeakable in his virtually limitless spare time.

We had roughly 540 valid family records in the Parish when I arrived. We sustained a net loss of 130 families because of failed pastoral leadership.

When you arrived, you were handed a wounded, bleeding congregation. Although the task of bringing healing and stability to this Parish that lay before you was huge, nonetheless, it was your obligation under your vocation to do so. My position was in place to allow you to do this without having to struggle with Parish business. You also used my position to disappear, Father. Your cold attitude and comments reflected that there was any place in the world that you would rather be than here, so you rarely were. You tended no flock, and reached out to virtually no one. You sent the same message to our faithful that

130

was sent from the Bishop and his people. The message was, "I really couldn't care less." More people left the Parish because they were not cared for. Whether from you or the Diocese, our people received absolutely no pastoral care whatsoever during this tragedy.

Then unfolding before your eyes since you came was an endless, cruel, and sinful campaign to malign my position and my personal character under your watch. How many times did I appeal to you and try to help you understand what was happening, who these people were, and why they were doing this? I gave peace a chance at every turn in the hope that this sin would cease. I appealed to the Diocese for their help simultaneously and was virtually ignored by all of you. A whistleblower was being relentlessly attacked in the Church, of all places, for having to stand up and protect the children and those who were in the position of authority who were supposed to be men of God stood by and simply watched. One would legitimately question whether this harassment had your "blessing." When strength was called for, only weakness could be found. When simply doing the right thing would solve so much, it was almost a given that the wrong thing would be chosen. When Bishop Martin was made aware of Father Thomas' dangerous activities on top of the McKinney complaint, He sent Father back to the Parish...and the children. I had to take action, hire legal counsel at my own expense and force the Bishop's hand to do the right thing and get this man away from the children. The very essence of the global clergy sex-abuse scandal was weakness, guilt, and cover up. Zero tolerance - what a complete farce!

We closed a $50,000 budget gap last year, and could have done so this year and you know it. I was terminated for budgetary reasons? Let's stop kicking the cow pie across the field and be honest. You are fully aware as to why I no longer have employment. The Bishop is fully aware as is Mr. Kurry and Msgr. Mira. I am no longer employed because of weakness, compromise, guilt, and indifference. My family no longer has means of support because so many men of the church have come to see themselves as princes rather than servants. I am no longer employed because Parishes are viewed as asset portfolios rather than outposts of pure grace. I am no longer employed because church leadership has forgotten love, propriety, and simple courage.

Shame on you Father. You were called to greatness and you settled for passive indifference.

I can have four months of pay if I sign a document releasing you and Diocesan officials from all accountability regarding your failure to lead and protect. I can have four months of health care for my family if I do the same. And you will write a letter saying nice things about me or as you proposed, I'll write it and you'll sign it, only if I deny all my rights to justice and full disclosure.
Once again, shame on you. For the love of God, shame on all of you.

Based upon my family's need, and your confidence that anyone in my desperate position would opt for money, insurance and a kind letter, you once again fail to honor your exalted positions. . I am rejecting your cold, corporate offer to purchase my silence. You seem to be forgetting something, gentlemen. I'm not like you.

Most Sincerely,

Patrick J. Flynn

.cc Bishop Martin
.cc Mark Kurry
.cc Msgr. Mira
.cc Robert Delisi

It would seem that the Diocese and Klanyi did have some strength after all, but only to do the wrong thing. In the meantime, under their leadership it would appear that predators and the liars who defend them are still protected and the innocent youth and their advocates are still in great danger.

"Faithless is he who says farewell when the road darkens."

J.R.R. Tolkien

Chapter Twelve

Failure of Leadership - Silence - The Mortal Sin of Cover up

The failure of leadership is responsible for the priest shortage which is now forcing the closing of Parishes and diminishing the work of Christ around the world. It is not celibacy or the exclusively male clergy. For many centuries the celibate male clergy policy was intact and vocations flourished. It has only been since the mid 1960's that sincere men hearing a vocational call have entered the seminaries, became horrified at what they saw and heard, and ran for the hills. It has only been since the mid 1960's that countless altar boys were molested and raped before they could even perceive a call to the sacrificial life. And, it has only been since the mid 1960's that the priest shortage developed and began damaging the church. It's a no-brainer.

The scandal in the church was obvious to everyone and was no longer being denied by church leadership by the year 2003. But what actually *is* the scandal and when did it start? This is argued to this day by church officials on all levels who wish to alter the dialog according to various levels of personal guilt. Many leaders in the church define the scandal as the exposition of the crisis by the media and others forcing the situation out from behind the shroud of secrecy. This conveniently seems to shift responsibility for the ensuing trouble onto the shoulders of witnesses, victims and the public. This aberration of truth is a disgusting attempt for the guilty to protect themselves. In reality of course, the scandal was none other than the revolting molestation of the innocent and the cover up performed by Bishops and cardinals. The timing of the scandal was not as they assert at the moment the public learned of the horror. It began long before that. The scandal occurred when the first priest laid his ill-intentioned hand on an innocent child and when the first Bishop moved such a man to a new location permitting him to accrue new victims.

Responsible authority over the offending individuals is the correct focus for assigning the most egregious failure in this crisis. The practical element of the scandal that made its way into the courtrooms and through the justice system is the sin of cover up, the well-crafted art of concealment and silence. The failure of leadership is the greater problem by far. The church and the faithful could have avoided so much pain and mortification by dealing directly and courageously with the bad seminaries, their corrupted rectors, and the clergy who began victimizing the innocent youth. Instead we saw the universal application of silence. We beheld outrageous instances of predator migration and denial. To make matters worse, misguided and often malicious faithful who were steeped in their own issues and determined to remain loyal to the perpetrators, fulfilled their role in the cover up by helping to target the victims, whistleblowers and accusers.

In this particular case the Diocese of Hamburg had been covering up for Father Thomas. Yes, Bishop Martin did ultimately remove Father and isolated him in his northern cottage. This was only done after I exerted the necessary pressure upon him. Up to that point and beyond, every effort was made to silence the whole affair across the home front. The Bishop's office refused to ever address the situation with Father Thomas either directly or indirectly. The Diocese would not answer any inquiries with valid information and appeared perfectly content to pretend the whole tragedy simply never happened.

In January of 2006, after Jude Devlock faxed his fraudulent account of the affair to the Parish, I contacted Mark Kurry to have the Diocese address these false rumors of Father Thomas' innocence. In response, the Diocese of Hamburg issued the following statement to be posted on the Parish website and published in the Parish bulletin. Fr. Klanyi was to simply attach his name to it:

> Father Wesley Thomas is on Administrative Leave.
>
> RUMORS AND INCOMPLETE INFORMATION are being circulated about Father Wesley Thomas. The Diocese of Hamburg is aware of this and, in fairness, cannot comment. They ask for your patience, understanding, and prayers. Let me continue the counsel I have consistently given since my arrival at Holy Cross Parish: Keep Father Thomas in your prayers along

with me and all priests. May God continue to bless our Parish and all who serve it.

-Fr. Steve Klanyi

The pathetic statement reflects the true spirit of cover up. While continuing to say nothing at all about Father Thomas and the real matter at hand, it asserts that anyone who is providing any information about him is unworthy of belief. The Diocese knew what I was being forced to reveal about Father Thomas was the truth. It simply made no difference to them. The goal was silence, cover up, and putting the Bishop and the Diocese in the best possible light. No truth would be given to the people by this Diocese and its leadership and no help would be afforded to victims of the scandal. After enough time passes in silence, people will begin to forget and nothing ever has to be done about it.

We now behold the true essence of the entire crisis - the failure of leadership, the scandal of cover up. Rather than acting as the supreme shepherd of his Diocese, this Bishop, and countless other Bishops around the world have failed their priests, their parishes, their families and God himself by refusing to address this horrendous tragedy with courage, resolve and charity. The result of this failure and indifference is the destruction of faith and vocations. The fruit of this negligence is that the church is now having to do all it can to close parishes, cluster faith communities and turn existing priests into burnt-out migrant workers serving multiple geographical parishes.

It is all because of the priest shortage, they cry. Why is there a priest shortage? Has God stopped calling young men to the sacrificial life of service to the church? Have men stopped hearing that call? Hardly. The truth is that we have a drastic reduction in the number of priests because of weakness, because of indifference, because of disobedience, because of false teaching, and because of the reprehensible moral evil of the raping of the innocent.

When seminaries flaunt and peddle erred teaching regarding sexuality and morality, we lose priests. When altar boys provide service to the church only to be violated by the very men who were responsible for inspiring them, we lose priests before they're even called. Now many Bishops are attempting to handle the shortage of priests without ever even acknowledging its real cause and their own responsibility for the defalcation. It is so sadly obvious. Water down the doctrine, pervert the seminaries, abuse the young men and in no time, you will have a serious priest shortage to deal with.

Chapter Thirteen
A Catholic Law School Augments the Scandal

In July of 2007, the website, AveWatch.com published a story alleging involvement of the Mother of God School of Law in the Father Thomas cover up. You will recall that Father Thomas had told the Chair of the Finance Council that he was receiving assistance from Mother of God. The story asserted that Father Pride, the Chaplain of the school, utilized the school's Information Technology Department to help Father Thomas in his efforts to manipulate and/or remove his computer hard drive. Since the onset of the whole affair, both Pride and the law school avoided all discussion on the topic and certainly gave the impression that they had nothing at all to do with Father's intent to deal with his computer drive. Fox2 News Detroit became involved and pressed the school's Dean, Bernard Forski until on July 20, the Dean issued the following statement:

> The basic allegation, in essence, is that the Law School, particularly through its Chaplain, Fr. Michael Pride, participated in helping a local Priest, who allegedly was accessing pornography on his computer, including possibly child pornography, to "clean," "scrub," "alter" and/or "remove" the hard drive from his computer.

> This outrageous allegation is absolutely and unequivocally false. Specifically, no employee of the Law School - including our Chaplain or any IT employee - was involved in the "cleaning," "scrubbing," or "removing" of the local Priest's computer hard drive. Moreover, there was never any conversation between the Priest in question and our Chaplain or any other Law School employee about how to "clean," "scrub," "alter" and/or "remove" the hard drive, or to assist in such efforts. Further, no Law School employee - including our Chaplain or any IT employee - ever handled, touched, or possessed the Priest's hard drive or computer. Any accusations to the contrary are false and completely unfounded.

> I want to emphasize that the above statements are based on facts disclosed to me during my initial investigation of the matter, and during two investigations directed by me and conducted by outside counsel. They are also based on facts reported to me from investigations conducted by multiple law enforcement

authorities, the local Diocese, and the Attorney Grievance Commission.

Briefly, this is what really happened. In late September 2005, the local Priest met with his Bishop about allegations that the Priest had been engaged in viewing internet pornography. During that meeting, the Priest reportedly was advised to remove "offensive material" from his computer. Later that same day, the Priest telephoned our Chaplain, who he previously knew, to advise him of the meeting with the Bishop and the allegations made against him, to proclaim his innocence, and to ask our Chaplain questions regarding the operations of a computer so that the Priest could establish his innocence of the charges. The Chaplain, unable to answer questions about computers, then asked a member of the Law School IT staff to talk to the Priest about how computers operate. At no time, however, did this conversation relate to cleaning, scrubbing, or otherwise replacing the hard drive. To the contrary, the conversation was about how information could be preserved on the computer hard drive - information which the Priest apparently believed would establish his innocence and might be lost forever if he took the advice he was given at the meeting to remove items from his hard drive - and not how to get rid of the information. **In other words, both our Chaplain and the IT employee were under the impression that the Priest was interested in maintaining a record of his internet activity, and not in destroying or altering that record.** To this end, the IT employee advised the Priest to seek technical assistance from the Diocese in preserving a record of his internet usage. Furthermore, and to the best of our knowledge, at the time that this conversation occurred there was no active police investigation involving the Priest. In fact, the Priest was told in the meeting with the Bishop, before his telephone conversation with our Chaplain and the IT employee, that county law enforcement officials, who had been asked to investigate the matter, would not be investigating it any further.

I can respond to these accusations directly and without equivocation because of the prompt and prudent steps that were institutionally undertaken by the Law School when I first learned about this matter. The allegation was initially brought to my attention by a Law School employee in December 2005, and I investigated it immediately. Despite the fact that I was satisfied after my own investigation that there was no wrongdoing by anyone at the Law School, I decided that an independent investigation would be desirable because of the seriousness of the matter involved. To that end, the Law School contracted with the Butzel Long law firm, one of the largest and most respected law firms in the state and a firm which has represented the Law School in the past. This law firm is very experienced in conducting investigations for corporations and academic institutions. As one example, this is the same law firm that recently was contracted by Eastern Michigan University to investigate the University's reporting of a campus murder, and whose investigation established that the reporting was not properly made.

Partners of the firm conducted for us an investigation in December 2005 and January 2006. After a thorough investigation, the investigators confirmed the facts I stated above and they also made several other findings. First, the hard drive on the Priest's computer had been replaced with a new one, and the old one given to someone else purportedly for safekeeping. None of these actions involved anyone at the Law School. Second, the original hard drive was turned over to the State Police. To the best information of the investigators, there was no evidence that the original hard drive was cleaned, scrubbed, or otherwise altered; rather, it was maintained intact. Finally, the outside investigation disclosed that the local Priest was advised in early October 2005, more than two weeks after his phone conversation with Law School personnel, that the Michigan Attorney General's office had begun an investigation. On November 30, 2005, the Diocese apparently was notified by the State Police that after its examination of the hard drive that had been removed, it would not be proceeding with a criminal prosecution, and the Diocese informed the local Priest of this the next day. As I indicated earlier, I first became aware of the September telephone call by the local Priest to the Law School in December 2005. Thus, to our best information, there was no criminal investigation occurring at the time I learned of the September call.

I make no judgment and express no opinion about whether the local Priest committed a crime or accessed pornography. This was not the purpose of our investigation. Rather, I directed the investigators to determine whether anyone at the Law School had done anything illegal or improper, **and whether we had an obligation to report anything to the authorities.** The investigators determined that no Law School employee had done anything illegal or improper. They also determined that the relevant authorities and entities - the State Police and the Diocese - had all the relevant information at the time that our

140

investigation was conducted. The State Police were aware that the original hard drive was replaced, and they had the opportunity to examine both the old and new hard drives, before any decision not to proceed with a criminal investigation. Likewise, the Diocese was fully aware of the circumstances surrounding the allegations made against the local Priest. For all of these reasons, the investigators advised me that the Law School had no obligation to report the innocuous September 2005 phone conversation about how computers track internet usage, particularly since that conversation concerned maintaining (and not destroying) a record of the Priest's computer usage.

In December 2006, I learned that the individual who made the original allegations against the local Priest with the Diocese had filed a Request for Investigation of the Priest's attorney with the Michigan Attorney Grievance Commission. The Request related to the attorney's role in the handling of the Priest's hard drive. I immediately asked the investigators who conducted our original investigation to look into the matter and determine whether any of the allegations made or materials submitted to the Grievance Commission in any way impacted on the conclusions that were reached in our previous investigation, conducted almost one year earlier. After investigating these additional matters, the investigators concluded that there was nothing in the later allegations or related materials that altered the original conclusion that no one at the Law School assisted the Priest in cleansing or otherwise altering his hard drive, or engaged in any other type of misconduct. They also indicated that they would re-visit the matter again if some action were to be taken against the attorney. It is now my understanding that the Grievance Commission has decided not to pursue the matter.

In closing, I want to emphasize that these most recent accusations against the Law School and its employees are incredibly serious and reckless, particularly when made in an attempt to link an innocent Priest such as our Chaplain with accusations involving possible child pornography. Much damage has been done to the reputation of the Law School over the past few years, and increasingly damage is now being done to the reputations of good and honorable people. I urge all those involved to cease engaging in senseless personal attacks because of the serious damage they inflict upon the Law School and members of our *community.*

The Dean's statement claims that the intent of the law school's assistance offered to Father Thomas was to preserve the computer drive. Ridiculous. Personal testimony and the results of the State Police investigation clearly exhibit intent to erase the offending drive. Indeed, after it was obtained through the issuance of search warrants, the drive did not profess Father's innocence. On the contrary, its content verified Father's sexual addiction and his possible possession of child pornography. Furthermore, the law school neglected to contact any legal authority at any time, even after they knew the Livingston County Prosecutor, Attorney General's office and State Police were conducting investigations, and then even after the ensuing police report revealed and documented the contents of the drive and the dire implications therein. Instead, they hired lawyers to affirm to them they were in no legal predicament. Mother of God School of Law is a Catholic entity. Their obligation first and foremost should have been the safety of innocent children. Then, at least they should have had grave concerns regarding any involvement on their part implying tampering with evidence and obstruction of justice. In reality, however, their primary concern, like that of so many Bishops and Diocesan officials around the world was to cover their self-righteous asses. Their silence says so much more than any exhaustive damage control statement ever could. This does not escape the notice of sincere Catholic law professionals:

> The Avewatch postings with respect to the alteration of the pastor's computer hard drive raise serious questions that ought to be answered in detail rather than in generalities. A prompt and thorough investigation should be made by an independent entity, with no connection to MGSL (Mother of God School of Law) or any of the parties involved, to determine whether any violations of law were committed in this matter. If any MGSL personnel, administrators or members of the Board of Governors knowingly performed or concealed illegal acts, they should resign.
>
> Charles E. Rice
> Professor Emeritus
> University of Notre Dame Law School

The law school's involvement with Fr. Thomas' computer was protested by several professors on the faculty. The professors believed their subsequent dismissal was partially a result of their opposition to the use of school resources in this manner. The men launched a lawsuit against the school and its leadership. The law school eventually settled with the plaintiffs.

Chapter Fourteen

A Bizarre Development

In July of 2007 Fox2 News contacted the Diocese. The reporter was referred to Michael Drake, the Director of Communications for the Diocese. The news asked Drake to comment on the allegations of Father Thomas' use of internet youth homosexual pornography. Drake told the reporter that Father Thomas was on leave of absence. He then lied to the media and told the reporter he had no knowledge of such allegations. The Fox2 reporter was alerted by Drake's claim which confirmed cover up. The reporter had a copy of the Michigan State Police report in his possession and the Diocese of Hamburg was listed as the complainant. Later that same day, Drake contacted the reporter with a carefully engineered statement to do some corporate damage control.

Later that month, while the Detroit media was investigating the cover up of Father Thomas and the Mother of God School of Law connection, I had heard from a Parishioner that one of Father Thomas' supporters had been circulating an email. It appeared Father went to Germany. The email stated that Father Thomas needed prayers because he was in a hospital there and had lapsed into a coma. On the morning of July 23, the reporter from Fox2 called me and informed me that according to reports, Father Thomas had apparently died during the night. The report of his death was verified later that day from the Diocese. We were told there would be a memorial service for him at the church but that he would be buried in Germany. It stuck me as rather odd that Father goes to Germany at the same time the media is trying to reach him for comment. How unusual also that an American citizen, an official priest of the Diocese of Hamburg who was born and maintained a home in Michigan would suddenly die and be buried in a foreign country. There is very little about Father Thomas' past, his life before and after ordination, his global migrations, his private behavior, and even his alleged death and burial that passes the smell test.

The memorial service offered by Bishop Martin took place at the church on July 27. The Bishop said nothing significant during the homily other than offering a history lesson about the founding of a religious order that Father Thomas once belonged to.

The worship aid published by the Diocese and handed out at the memorial service mentioned that Father Thomas was "granted" a leave of absence from his duties in October of 2005. This is a deception. It gives the illusion that Father willingly sought a period of dismissal and the Diocese approved. In reality, as we know Father was removed from the Parish and his duties against his will after I forced the Bishop's hand. Father actually retained a Canon Lawyer to begin action against the Diocese to protest his removal. Deceptions such as this are engineered to sanitize the situation. They are elements of cover up.

The handout also contained a timeline of Fr. Thomas' life and career. In August of 1999 right after Fr. Thomas' arrival at Holy Cross, our Parish secretary received a call from a staff member at the Missionary church he had just left in McLean, Virginia. The caller, quite upset told the secretary that Father ruined the finances at the church and stole the checkbook when he left. Interestingly, the year or so Father served at that church in Virginia was curiously missing from the timeline.

After the Mass, Bishop Martin made his quick exit forgoing the free luncheon and cowardly avoided having to personally confront his flock.

Of the approximately forty priests who were in attendance at the memorial service, only one of them approached me to offer compassion and kindly inquire about my family's welfare. Other than this one priest, there were two others who, at different times offered their prayers and help. Three out of forty. That sadly is a fairly accurate indicator for the current state of our church.

Chapter Fifteen
Residual Pain and Dysfunction

As in most cases where someone in the position of authority is caught doing something terrible and then denies it, we find people confused, heartbroken, and angry. Healing is virtually impossible when the perpetrator renounces the humility to account for his actions. Peace is only possible if all concerned seek it. In the situation at Holy Cross, the pain endures. Although many new names have filled various leadership roles, the wounds still remain open, and the Parish in its suffering still bears the remains of a dark mystery.

On September 16, 2007 A Parish assembly was convened. Roughly 120 people were present when the news broke of a new Pastor possibly being assigned within weeks. Word had it that he was a good man who really wanted to be at Holy Cross despite the conflict. Mrs. Panky took the opportunity at the event to do her part to prevent this healing. She rose to the podium and lied to the people exclaiming Father Thomas' innocence and persecution. A good portion of the audience responded to the continuation of her filthy agenda with applause.

Of course, proper leadership would go a long way in pulling this Parish through its ordeal. Unfortunately if men like Bishop Martin, Monsignor Mira, Mark Kurry, and Father Klanyi, are responsible for continued leadership, it isn't likely. That's because they all care about the wrong things. There is always hope that the new Pastor can triumph in his leadership. That remains to be seen.

At Holy Cross Parish, there was no real healing to speak of. Gossip and insinuations ruled the talk pockets after Mass. It certainly didn't help when Fr. Pride directly participated in the suspicions and character assassinations injecting his poison into the ears of the unsuspecting. The sign of peace rite at Mass for many was disingenuous as people who were once rather close friends openly sneered and condemned one another. Some in the Parish were still actively fostering the illusion of mysteriously "missing and stolen" money. Tragically, some of the most cruel and malicious people can often be found in church pews deceptively draped with the concealing shroud of false piety.

In the summer of 2007, Holy Cross learned that indeed a new pastor would be assigned to the Parish. Father Klanyi could now breathe easier. He would soon be able to drop the marginal façade of his care for our church and run like hell from the accountability of leadership. There was a pathetic farewell event planned for Father Klanyi. It was predictably a total exercise of symbolism over substance complete with cards, handshakes, trinkets from the gift shop, photo opportunities and fantasy tales of how he led all of us through a bad time all bolstered by silly and completely uncalled for applause.

Will the new pastor understand what is happening? Will he show the leadership necessary to effect healing? Will he listen with the discerning heart of a loving shepherd? Will he educate himself with documented facts to ward off the many lies? He will be approached by allied groups of scandal makers vying to influence him. Will he allow them to put themselves back into positions of Parish influence and further their agenda? Has the Diocese already poisoned the truth in his ears? We'll see.

Chapter Sixteen
The Parishioners – A Study of Character and Roles

Circumstances like these for a parish become defining moments for each member in some way. Some of the ways different people reacted in this case are worth noting, because surely human nature dictates these same characters and reactions are common to all cases of abusing clergy and leadership cover up. Observe the roles below. Perhaps they can be of assistance in understanding the human condition and its critical response to crisis and pain. Hopefully their disclosure can play some small part in the ultimate resolution of this tragedy.

The Silent Majority

Firstly, there are great majorities who will not completely know or care about what the details of parish "internal works" are. So long as Mass is offered and uninterrupted, all is well with them. Sounds like a happy place to be! But it does not foster holiness or evangelization. The trials occurring in our Holy Mother Church right now should be borne by all. It is unjust to let only some bear the weight of this burden. God wants us to intensify and deepen our faith by means of the cross. Offending clergy were moved around so easily from parish to parish during the 60's, 70's, 80's and 90's because the laity was asleep. It is unacceptable today for us to remain lethargic.

In the opening paragraphs of *The Decree on the Apostolate of the Laity*, Pope Paul VI tells us:

> An indication of this manifold and pressing need (for the activity of the laity) is the unmistakable work being done today by the Holy Spirit in making the laity ever more conscious of their own responsibility and encouraging them to serve Christ and the Church in all circumstances.

Note that serving is indicated *for all circumstances*. We do not have an "out" when the Church is in crisis. Likewise, the document states:

> No part of the structure of a living body is merely passive but has a share in the functions as well as life of the body: so, too, in the body of Christ, which is the Church, "the whole body . . . in keeping with the proper activity of each part, derives its increase from its own internal development" (Eph. 4:16)

> Indeed, the organic union in this body and the structure of the members are so compact that the member who fails to make his proper contribution to the development of the Church must be said to be useful neither to the Church nor to himself.

And at the end of this document, the exhortation:

> The most holy council, then, earnestly entreats all the laity in the Lord to answer gladly, nobly, and promptly the more urgent invitation of Christ in this hour and the impulse of the Holy Spirit. Younger persons should feel that this call has been directed to them especially and they should respond to it eagerly and generously. Through this holy synod, the Lord renews His invitation to all the laity to come closer to Him every day, recognizing that what is His is also their own (Phil. 2:5), to associate themselves with Him in His saving mission. Once again He sends them into every town and place where He will come (cf. Luke 10:1) so that they may show that they are co-workers in the various forms and modes of the one apostolate of the Church, which must be constantly adapted to the new needs of our times. Ever productive as they should be in the work of the Lord, they know that their labor in Him is not in vain (cf. 1 Cor. 15:58).

If you are one who has examined himself and have found that you are indeed uninvolved in your parish life, please take the time to read the entire document of *The Decree on the Apostolate of the Laity*, which can be found at www.vatican.va. We are all needed. Together let us renew our baptismal vows, take up our crosses, be filled with the Holy Spirit and renew the face of the earth!

Perhaps the next largest group is made up of those who know the workings of the Parish and the persons involved but don't want to be "put in the middle". Some common comments have been "I'm not taking sides," "I'm staying out of this." "I have friends in both camps and I don't want to lose any friends." One day at Holy Cross, one of the teachers in the school came into my office and told me, "thank you so much for what you have done for our children but I hope you understand I just cannot be seen with you."

Are there really two sides to every story? Does one side have just as much merit as the other? Are all things open to debate?

If you stare at an object with one eye opened at a time, alternating eyes, you will see that the item looked upon appears to move, though it has not indeed done so. But, in fact in *truth* it is in one place. You would be best served to find out where this object truly is. Likewise, concerning events of the magnitude of the clergy sex abuse scandal, you would be best served to find out what really happened. There is truth, and there are lies. Perception alone is not good enough. There is simply too much at stake.

Here is a little modern-day parable for those whose character falls into this category:

> There is a bank in town that many people patronize. The bank's president is well liked and professional, as bankers go. He is so admired that people drive as far as an hour away to come to his bank. He is conservative and provides many of the "perks" that customers want in a bank including good interest rates, loans, "conservative" money management. In fact, not only do the customers appreciate the president, but so do the employees.

> One day, the head teller, also well respected by all, notices some money is missing. She can't imagine how such a large sum could possibly have disappeared. No one had access to it except for employees. She keeps her eyes open, feeling a deep sense of concern, sadness and internal upset. One day, as she came in unexpectedly to pick up her paycheck, she saw the president throw a money sack into his car trunk and slam it shut.

She felt utterly sick to her stomach. How could this be? She loved and respected her boss. So did the whole community! Why did "she" have to be the one to see this?

With deep regret, she talks to the police. The police seize the security tapes, and sure enough, there is the hard evidence.

Now, despite the evidence, the president denies his guilt. In fact, perhaps he claims or insinuates the head teller took the money, framed him and altered the video.

Where are the two sides? There is the truth, substantiated by the evidence and there is a ridiculous counter claim which defies reason.

There are no sides to this. This is not a debate. This is a vital moment in both the eternal realm and our present moment. The implications of this can include destruction of lives, unimaginable suffering and eternal judgment. Based upon what you know, you will be accountable before God for your action or inaction. If you behold great evil, you are required to respond accordingly. Make no mistakes, the destruction of the innocent and cover up are great evils. They are great evils when committed by lay people. They are so much more horrific and disgusting when committed by clergy.

The Low Energy Supporters

There will be many in the Parish who accept the truth supported by evidence. They will pledge strong support and defend the position of the victim or in this case the whistleblower. In most cases these will be friends who begin to share their own concerns regarding Father in one way or another. Early in the conflict their valuable support can be counted on and greatly appreciated. The duration of strong support, however, will wane as the cost rises. The wiles of the self-deceived and the depraved Parishioners detailed below increasingly augment the tension in the Parish and low energy support begins to diminish. It gets too difficult for these people to continue in their defense. They grow weary of the conflict and begin longing for the time when it was much easier to be a parishioner.

151

The Self-Deceived

This can include many Parishioners who simply cannot or will not believe that Father is anything but a saint. They will actually begin to bolster their position now that he is "persecuted" like the saints of old. No amount of evidence or testimony suffices to move them from their denial. As detailed in chapter Five, the reasons people assume this role are varied. It may be due to unresolved personal issues. It may stem from a strong historical blind trust for clergy and positions of church leadership. It may have its basis in real fondness for the offending priest or bishop. Still it may stem from deeply imbedded emotional or psychological distress as in the case of our Teresa Panky evidenced by her cruel and anti-social behavior.

A personal history of sexual abuse is a considerable factor in how people may behave. Whereas it may trigger instant rage against the guilty priest, it may also augment denial as some people are simply unable or unwilling to believe they are faced with yet another event of abuse. Remember, seven of the Parishioners who signed the letter to the Bishop seeking Fr. Thomas' return had personal experiences with sexual abuse in one form or another. In this case, the vast majority of the self-deceived were fairly close friends prior to the crisis.

The Depraved

It is difficult to imagine the free choice for pure evil. Some cannot believe that people ever really do this. There are even clergy that proclaim the heresy of the non existence of mortal sin. In our case at Holy Cross and in virtually every other case of parish sin and cover up there are those who are fully aware of the truth yet possess both the influence and the skills to manipulate the dynamics of the event. In this case, it really cannot be argued this is the character and intent of Jude Devlock. For whatever reason, he after knowing the truth shamefully lied and defamed in an attempt to manipulate the outcome of this tragedy. The depraved are without a doubt the most dangerous people in these stories aside from the molesters. Among the ranks of the depraved are often bishops and other diocesan leaders. The filthy work of their hands permits the ongoing destruction of innocence.

The Courageous

We must admit, if not for the rock solid commitment to truth and justice of several parishioners, my family quite possibly could have been overwhelmed by the horror and pain of this parish catastrophe, this crash-and-burn devastation of faith, trust, career and friendship. We remained parishioners at Holy Cross due to the love and courage of these people. They defended the truth. They calmly presented the facts to others when challenged. They gently led others as much as possible to the realization of Father's sad situation and his irreconcilable explanations. They stood and protested the unjust treatment by the self-deceived and the depraved at council meetings and Parish functions. They consoled us and understood our pain. They prayed for us, for resolution, for Father and even for the true enemies of the Church. I was indeed blessed that the majority of the parish staff were part of this group. As friends they drew our family closer as if to offer their mere proximity as a shelter from the suffering we were being forced to endure. They were and are the image of God in this often godless experience. Their holiness is of the variety that has sustained Christianity for over 2000 years.

Chapter Seventeen
Lessons Learned

It is a question as old as the human experience itself following a great trial. "What have you learned from this?" In this particular case and as a local chapter in the global clergy sex abuse crisis, the answers are not simple. The answers will depend on whom you are asking. What lessons have I learned personally from this? What has Laura learned? What have our children learned? How about our parish, the clergy, the Bishop, the Catholic Church at large, all of Christianity, all of humanity?

We can only honestly speak of the lessons learned up to this point in time for all of the above. This is far from complete as an experience. The lessons learned 25 years from now regarding the crisis will most likely be more relevant having the benefit of the development of time and retrospective observation.

For Laura and me personally, we have learned a few lessons indeed. We have learned that we do a great disservice when we venerate living human beings. We have learned that giving anything to man which God alone deserves is a plan for great suffering and a violation of the First Commandment. We have learned that humility and honesty always trump pride and deception. We have learned that we are passionate, fallible, and far from perfect. We have learned that wartime and peacetime human behavior has its differences for better or for worse. We have learned that for outer, visible peace to exist, all have to seek it or else there will be no peace. We have learned that you can still love people you cannot stand. We have learned that there is a great difference between the Holy Church and the occasionally unholy people entrusted with her care. We have learned that priests are as capable as anyone else of great holiness and great sin. We have learned that at least in the present time, many church officials unfortunately cannot be trusted. We have learned that confiding in a diocesan attorney at the onset is a huge mistake. We should have gone straight to the police upon discovery thus pre-empting what happens to be the willful cover up of the Diocese. We have learned that suffering hurts and often times does not subside when we try to pray it away. We have learned that the truth is not always welcome, sought, recognized, embraced, enjoyed, or appreciated by everyone. We have learned that tyranny is the potential byproduct of any human authority. We have learned that goodness, although present can be very difficult to see during painful times. We have learned that justice is a guarantee only in Heaven and is not always available to everyone in this world.

Our children have learned that Jesus is still present in His suffering Church. They have learned that people who are supposed to be really good sometimes behave very badly. They have learned that feelings and inner struggles can cause friends to misunderstand. They have learned that unfortunately some people that you believed to be friends can be anything but. They have learned that their mom and dad love them immensely and will undertake any necessary sacrifices to protect them. They have learned that God loves them and wants them to seek and defend justice and mercy even when it is denied. They hopefully will learn how to forgive by understanding how we are forgiven.

For our Parish, the question of lessons learned is difficult. Some in the Parish have learned great lessons about remaining quiet and prayerful if you don't know all the facts. Many have not learned this lesson. Some in the Parish have learned that outward signs, rituals and spiritual words are not necessarily elements of holiness. Some have missed this lesson completely. Some have learned that strength and orthodoxy can be violated and used as a veil to cover great depravity. Some still cling to symbolism over substance. Some have learned the lesson that our fears can limit our love and drive others away. Some are perfectly fine with never having to learn that.

The clergy and other church leadership should have learned that they will be held accountable, and that trust and respect must be earned and not simply demanded. There is sadly a strong indication, however, that many of the priests and the Bishops have learned nothing at all aside from being careful. Not one church leader involved in the Church and the scandal at Holy Cross including Bishop Martin, Msgr. Mira, Msgr. Benke, Deacon Kurry,

Fr. Klanyi, Deacon Boehman or Fr. Thomas has offered an apology for what this outrage has done to my family. Of course we know what they care most about, therefore, apologies could legally complicate things. Therefore, victims and those who step forward to hold sinful men accountable are still harassed and considered enemies of the Church to this day.

Considering the whole of the Catholic Church, the remainder of Christianity, and all of humanity, it's too early to assess. One thing I believe we will all learn is that Jesus' promise regarding the Church in Matthew 16:18 and its withstanding the gates of Hell is true and one way or another God will deal with this horrible crisis and the Church will experience victory.

So where do we and the myriad of other parishes rocked by scandal go from here? How do we get beyond all of this? First, we realize and accept what has happened. Then we *come to terms*. We come to terms with the fact that the past cannot be undone. We honestly identify the many levels of failure in this global scandal and speak the truth. We come to terms that on a large scale, the Catholic Church throughout the world is suffering through one of the worst trials in her 2000 year history. We come to terms with the fact that the priest shortage has been caused by failed leadership, bad teaching and poor example rather than celibacy. We come to terms with the fact that for decades in the 60's, 70's and 80's, many men who were suffering with same sex attraction and broken personal lives who were in desperate need of pastoral care were given the keys to the church. We come to terms with the reality that these men fed off of each other's problems and justified each other's sin. We come to terms with the fact that by now many of these broken men have reached the official levels of bishop and cardinal with secrets in their pasts that compromise pastoral leadership. We come to terms with the fact that a large part of church leadership has violated our trust and in so many cases destroyed the lives of our young men. We understand and accept the reality that joining the guilty in their denial and enabling their continued sin is a violation of the virtue of Charity. We take stock of all we have lost, and what we can salvage. We tell the truth courageously regardless of whom it embarrasses. We stop

156

making excuses and refuse to cooperate with silence and cover up. We are honest in telling our children that the church leadership has let them down. We plead with them to keep their faith in Christ Jesus. We pray and work for justice. We forgive while demanding accountability. We learn good lessons to ensure that these tragic events initiate real efforts of prevention. And we frequent the Sacraments and plead God's mercy for what we have done to his bride and to his innocent children.

Chapter Eighteen
A Quest for Resurrection

In this dark time, the collateral damage to the faithful and to all of humanity is considerable. So many have left the Catholic Church because of the reprehensible sin of her clergy and the damnable cover up by her leaders. This global scandal has become fuel for anti-Catholic and anti-religious individuals and groups. In some situations, victims and/or their loved ones no longer believe there is a God. If you consider the immense pain, injustice and revictimization endured by these people, can you really blame them?

For me, it is different. I will not turn from the Catholic Faith despite my struggle. I have been able to complete a separation in my mind and heart. I refuse to associate the perfect divine handiwork of Jesus Christ with the reprehensible sins of the many sick and depraved men who now hold the Church hostage on earth. Predators, their sympathizers and defenders will not steal my faith. In an oddly refreshing and renewed way, my worship is now much more simple and pure, free from the praise and adoration of human beings.

Obviously nothing that is done can be undone. Healing will not come with new policies and programs designed to stroke the faithful and the media. It will certainly not come through the United States Conference of Catholic Bishops and their empty promises to guard the hen house. Healing will need to be a courageous decision by God's faithful combined with fearless accountability.

Despite all the pain and suffering, I believe in Easter Sunday. I believe in open tombs. I believe in the sunrise for the cause and mission of Christianity in the world. Until that time, we are on a quest. It is a quest for truth and justice. It is a quest for God's divine touch. It is a quest for fulfillment of man's journey to salvation. It is indeed a quest for resurrection.

It is, after all, Christ's unfathomable mercy, justice and divine protection that has shed light on all this darkness. This exposing of great sin in the Church should be considered a gift and a sign.

Christ has died. Christ is risen. Christ will come again. And His bride, the Church will be prepared.

Maranatha!

Notes:

1. From the article, *The Liturgical Impact of Homosexuality in the Priesthood*, Louie Verrecchio
2. Father did not specify at the time which of the many Mother of God entities he was referring to.
3. Canon 1717, se. 2
4. *"Homosexual Orientation is not a "Gift."* A copy of the article was included in the monthly Roman Catholic Diocese of Lansing Courage and Encourage Newsletter. The article originally appeared on the Women for Faith and Family website, Novembeer, 2005.

38127154R00097

Made in the USA
Middletown, DE
13 December 2016